PUFFIN BOOKS

LITTLE BADMAN

AND THE
TIME-TRAVELLING TEACHER
OF DOOM

HUMZA ARSHAD & HENRY WHITE
Illustrated by ALEKSEI BITSKOFF

PUFFIN

PUFFIN BOOKS

UK | USA | Canada | Ireland | Australia
India | New Zealand | South Africa

Puffin Books is part of the Penguin Random House group of companies
whose addresses can be found at global.penguinrandomhouse.com.

www.penguin.co.uk
www.puffin.co.uk
www.ladybird.co.uk

First published 2020

001

Text copyright © Big Deal Films Ltd, 2020
Illustrations copyright © Aleksei Bitskoff, 2020

BIG DEAL FILMS

The moral right of the authors and illustrator has been asserted

Set in 13/18pt Bembo

Printed in Great Britain by Clays Ltd, Elcograf S.p.A.

A CIP catalogue record for this book is available from the British Library

ISBN: 978–0–241–37850–2

All correspondence to:
Puffin Books
Penguin Random House Children's
One Embassy Gardens, 8 Viaduct Gardens,
London SW11 7BW

I'd like to dedicate this to my beautiful wife, who I still haven't found yet. My parents, because I feel that they would want me to say that. Team Badman, my loyal crazy fans. And most importantly, God! — Humza

To my mum and dad, who made childhood funny, even when it wasn't — Henry

CHAPTER ONE
AGENT BADMAN

Let me get straight to the point, yeah. I'm a pretty big deal. It's just that no one knows it but me. Why? Cos I've got to keep it all a secret. And it ain't no small secret either, like when I set fire to my mum's wedding dress while trying to cook salad (though that is still a secret, so maybe don't mention it). This stuff is proper top-secret secret. I shouldn't even be writing it down.

But if I don't tell someone I reckon I'll go crazy, like my dad. He ain't got no secrets or nothin' – he was just born that way. Seriously, he once made me eat a book as a punishment. Who does that?

Anyway, point is, I'm massively unappreciated, all because I can't tell anyone how amazing I am.

Actually, that ain't true. I tell a lot of people how amazing I am. They just don't believe me, cos I can't tell 'em why. Like, for instance, did you know, earlier this year, I saved the Earth from alien invaders? That's pretty impressive, right?

Actually, you know what? If you ain't heard that story, you've got some serious catching up to do. Luckily, I just so happen to be a world-class rapper. So how about I bust out a quick lyrical recap? Kinda like one of those 'Previously on . . .' things that you get on TV shows, but this time delivered by Eggington's greatest living freestyler. Here goes:

**This is the story of what went down,
the day that the aliens rolled through my town.
All of the teachers at school disappeared,
replaced by aunties, acting weird.**

**Aunties everywhere, feeding us like crazy;
kids getting overweight, tired and lazy –
turned out to be an invasion plan.
Someone had to save the day – *Little Badman*!**

Big fat space slugs starting trouble,
brainwashing aunties to feed us double,
stretching our tummies so they could move in.
You can't fit a space slug if you're too thin.

Looks like a job for the Badman crew:
Wendy, Umer and Grandpa too.
Slugs sent packing, back to the sky.
Saved Planet Earth, so they made me a spy!

How's that for some tight lyrics? Three hundred action-packed pages, smashed into sixteen bars. As you can tell, it was a pretty big couple of weeks in Eggington. That's my hood by the way. And proper dangerous it is too. Kind of like gangland LA, but even deadlier. Seriously, I once got chased for three blocks by a goose, just for chucking acorns at him. If that ain't gangsta, I don't know what is.

Anyway, cos I did such a good job fighting off those aliens, I got recruited by this top-secret spy organization called the Agency. When they found out what I'd done, they made me a spy in training. That's right, me! I was about to become the Asian James Bond. The brown Jason Bourne. The Muslim Inspector Gadget. And about time too – my skills were wasted at school.

Problem was, nothing happened. Seriously, not one phone call. Not one mission. Where was my training? Where was my licence to kill? Where were all my spy gadgets? I didn't even have a proper mobile phone!

And that's where this story begins. Twelve years old, one week into my summer holidays, and forced to use my dad's rubbish old Nokia to ring Agent Akbar . . .

'Hello?' said the deep voice at the other end of the line.

'Yo yo yo, wagwan, Agent Akbar?' I replied.

'Humza, is that you?'

'Yeah, bro, long time no speak.'

'You phoned me this morning.'

'Yeah, but it feels like longer, cos of our good relationship.'

'As I keep telling you.' Agent Akbar sighed. 'None of this happens overnight. The Agency will make contact with you when we are ready. This line is for emergencies only.'

'This is an emergency, man! I'm bored. If I'm gonna be a world-famous spy, I'm gonna need a mission.'

'There are no world-famous spies, Humza. That is the point. We are a secret organization.'

'You know what I mean. If I'm one of you now, you've gotta give me something to get my teeth into!'

'But you are not one of us yet. You are still in training.'

'But you ain't given me no training!'

'Have patience.'

'Like a doctor?'

'No, that's spelled differently.'

'Come on, man, *please*. This is torture!'

'When the time is right, we will contact you.

Until then, get on with your life. Enjoy your summer.'

'But –'

'I promise it will be soon,' interrupted Agent Akbar.

'Yeah, OK,' I groaned, not bothering to hide my frustration. 'But don't forget or I'll just call you again.'

'Yes, I imagine you will. Goodbye, Humza.'

'You mean *Agent Badman*.'

'What?' he replied, sounding confused.

'I figure I need a code name, like 007. Agent Badman's got a pretty good ring to it, right?'

'*Goodbye*, Humza,' he said wearily.

'Yeah, OK then,' I replied, and hung up.

As soon as I did, there came a booming voice from behind me.

'*HUMZA!!!*'

'Aargh!' I yelled, spinning round.

'Is that my phone?' demanded my dad, staring at the little red Nokia I was holding.

'What, this old thing?' I replied, looking innocent. 'Nah, probably just a coincidence. We must shop at the same Poundland.'

'Give me that!' he snarled, snatching it out of my

hand. 'If I catch you using my phone again, I will glue your hands to your feet, drop you into a barrel of daal, and ship you straight to Pakistan.'

'Why d'you even keep threatening me with that? We both know Mum ain't ever gonna let you ship me off to Pakistan.'

'Nonsense! She said I could not send you *in a crate*. She said nothing about a barrel!'

'Whatever. There ain't no way I'm going to Pakistan while Mum's got a say in it!'

'Don't count on it, boy! You keep acting like a hooligan and sooner or later she will come round to the idea!'

'Who you calling a hooligan?'

'Ha!' My dad laughed. 'Who do you think? Stealing my phone? Breaking my windows? Trapping a seagull in the kitchen?'

'Hey! That ain't fair! That was the seagull's fault!'

'You have been trouble since the day you were born. I have told your mother: you need discipline! Pakistan is the only place you will receive a proper upbringing!'

'What, like you did?' I said, and now it was my turn to laugh. 'Yeah, right! Just yesterday I saw you use a cat as a napkin!'

'He enjoyed it!' shouted my dad. 'He was smiling.'

'Cats can't smile!' I shouted back.

'Cats *can* smile!' he shouted, even louder.

'You're impossible!' I said, throwing my hands up.

'*You're* impossible!' he replied.

'Right, I'm leaving!' I said, storming towards the front door.

'Good!' he yelled.

'Good!' I yelled back.

Man, I was fuming by the time I walked through the park gates. And, thanks to my run-in with Pakistan's angriest man, I was late now too. That was five minutes of valuable tree-climbing time that I'd missed out on. Didn't my dad realize that my holiday was only six weeks long? Every minute I spent talking to him was a minute not spent having fun.

'Why so grumpy?' said Umer as I marched up to the tree he and Wendy were hanging from.

'*I* ain't grumpy. *You're* grumpy,' I replied grumpily.

'Maybe you're a *bit* grumpy?' suggested Wendy, dropping to the ground beside me.

'Yeah, OK, maybe a bit,' I grumbled. 'It's just my stupid dad. I can't believe he doesn't remember anything that happened last month.'

'Well,' replied Wendy, sliding her glasses back up her nose after her jump, 'the Agency *did* wipe his memory.'

'And everyone else's,' added Umer.

'I know,' I said, kicking a tuft of grass loose with my toe. 'I just thought some of it might have stuck, deep in that thick skull of his. I mean, we *did* save the world, after all. That ain't exactly *small*.'

'If it helps, my mum doesn't remember anything either,' said Wendy.

'Yeah, but your mum already liked you. My dad treats me like something the dog threw up.'

'I didn't know you had a dog,' replied Umer.

'What?' I said, turning to him, confused.

'Your dog. You said he threw up.'

'It ain't a real dog!' I snapped.

'Oh . . .' said Umer, looking lost. 'So why did your pretend dog throw up?'

'It didn't!' I yelled. 'There is no dog! I was just making a point about . . . Oh, forget it!'

Man, I tell you, sometimes Umer winds me right up. It ain't his fault – it's just how his brain works.

I mean, he may not be the sharpest prong on the fork, but he ain't stupid either. He's just kind of . . . Umer. What can I say? He's my oldest friend. I've known him since I was the size of a bag of rice and he was the size of a slightly bigger, less attractive bag of rice. I know him so well that I can tell what he's thinking before he's even said it (usually cos he's thinking about his next meal and I can hear his tummy rumbling). But, like I say, he's my best mate.

Here are a few reasons why:
1. He makes me laugh (sometimes even on purpose).
2. He can eat an entire family bucket from Uzbek Fried Chicken without being sick.
3. He's twelve but he still says 'hoskiple' instead of 'hospital'.
4. He never told anyone about the time I cried during *The Avengers*.
5. He's probably the nicest person I've ever met. You know, the kind of niceness you normally only get with grandmas and school nurses. He's like a chubby little Gandhi. Everyone should have an Umer.

Wendy, on the other hand, had basically been my enemy until about six weeks ago. Before I knew her properly, I'd have probably called her an egghead or a 'brainiac' – good at school, hard-working, never in trouble. Obviously, this meant that she and I could never be friends. Or at least that's what I'd thought, until those alien slugs came along. There's nothing like an extraterrestrial invasion to bring people together. And, if it hadn't been for Wendy, we'd have never beaten those nasty green slime-sacks and saved the world. Turns out, as well as being the smartest person I've ever met, she's also seriously brave and a ton of fun. She just needed some practice bending the rules, and I was happy to lend a hand.

Anyway, the three of us had been through a lot together recently. That's why it felt so bad not telling them about the whole trainee-secret-agent thing. See, the problem was, the Agency had only chosen me. They'd made me swear not to tell a soul – not even my best friends.

But, man, I hated lying to them. I mean, don't get me wrong – I love lying to Umer when it's funny. I once convinced him that his cat's fur would grow back overnight if he shaved it all off with his dad's beard trimmer. For the next two months it looked like he owned a massive purring rat. Normally, though, my world-class lying skills are reserved for my parents, or teachers, or anyone in a position of authority – you know, people I actually *want* to lie to. Keeping something from my two best friends sucked.

It turns out I wasn't the only one with something to hide though. Wendy had been keeping a secret of her own, which slipped out halfway up the tree.

'Maths camp?' I spluttered, staring down at her. 'What the hell is maths camp?'

'It's a camp where you do maths,' said Wendy from a few branches below.

'That sounds terrible. Why would you go there during your summer holidays? It's the one time of the year you *don't* have to do maths!'

'My parents arranged it months ago,' she replied. 'It was before we all started hanging out together. And, anyway, I like maths.'

'I'm sure it'll be great,' said Umer, who was hanging upside down, so all the blood had gone to his big bowling-ball head.

'Damn it, man! Why are you supporting this?' I shouted at him. 'We had major plans this summer.

The three of us hanging out, teaching Wendy how to misbehave. Now it's ruined.'

'We can still hang out,' replied Wendy. 'For a few more days at least.'

'Man, if my parents sent me to maths camp, I'd divorce them,' I muttered, shaking my head.

'Come on, guys,' said Umer, flipping himself over to hang by his arms. 'We'll just have to make the most of the time we've got. Put every single minute to really good use.'

'Yeah? Doing what, exactly?' I asked.

'Ring and run?' suggested Umer.

'What's "ring and run"?' asked Wendy.

'It's when you ring someone's doorbell and run away,' he explained.

'Why would anyone want to do that?' replied Wendy, who'd obviously never experienced the thrill of being chased down the street by a stranger whose bell you've just rung for the sixth time in twenty minutes.

'Ah, Wendy Wang,' I said as I clambered down to pat her on her shoulder, 'there are some things they just don't teach you at maths camp.'

And, with that, we climbed out of the tree and set off to annoy anyone who had a doorbell.

CHAPTER TWO
SCHOOL SUCKS

'*You are in so much trouble, you will wish you woke up dead!*' shouted my dad as I walked through the front door.

What the hell? Most kids come home to '*Hi, darling, how was your day?*' I come home to *that*!

'What? It was only a few doorbells!' I yelled.

'Doorbells?' shouted my dad. 'What are you talking about?'

That's when I spotted the policeman standing behind him.

Uh-oh . . .

This was serious. The police don't show up for no reason. And if it wasn't ring-and-run, what could it be? I was racking my brain to think of anything I'd done that was bad enough to make the cops get involved, but I couldn't come up with a thing. I'd been pretty well behaved lately. In fact, since being offered a job with a top-secret agency of super spies, I'd been on my best behaviour. I didn't want to risk blowing it before it had even begun.

'Hello, Humza,' said the copper.

Ah, man, I totally recognized this guy. I'd met him a few months back, during the whole alien-invasion bit. He'd said the police had a file on me because I was a nuisance. He'd basically called me a liar because I kept trying to warn the police about serious threats to Eggington. Stuff like vampires and werewolves and that super-intelligent guinea pig at the petting zoo. Yeah, fine, none of those things turned out to be as real as I'd thought at the time. But the aliens had been. And if it hadn't been for me they'd have taken over the world. Problem was, since the Agency wiped everyone's minds to cover it up, the only ones who remembered were me, Umer, Wendy – and Grandpa.

I'll tell you more about Grandpa in a bit. For now, all you need to know is that he ain't my grandpa, he's my uncle – Dad's big brother. Everyone just calls him Grandpa because he looks about a thousand years old and always has done. But that's what made him such a great secret agent. When you're *that* grey and wrinkly, no one would ever suspect you're a spy. It was like he was invisible. He slipped under everybody's radar.

They probably just thought he was some confused old geezer who'd wandered off from his care home without permission. But, the truth is, even though he looks old, his mind's as sharp as ever. And without his help we'd have never saved the day from those evil space slugs. Anyway, you'll meet him properly soon.

Until then, back to the police . . .

'Hello, officer,' I said, giving him my best innocent smile. 'How are you on this fine summer's afternoon?'

I must have been nervous cos I ain't never talked like that in my life.

'We're here to talk to you about an act of graffiti at the primary school,' he replied, looking seriously annoyed.

'Eh? What graffiti?'

'I thought that's what you might say,' he said unimpressed. 'That's why we brought these.' He pulled out a stack of photographs and held them up for me to see.

As I reached to take them, he snatched them away. 'Hey! Hands off!' he snapped. 'These are evidence.'

'Evidence? Of what? I ain't done nothing.'

'Oh really?' growled my dad. 'We have photos this time!'

I looked at the top picture. It was clearly taken from a CCTV camera, all black-and-white and grainy, and there was a figure in the shot. Whoever it was, they were halfway through graffitiing a wall with a can of spray paint. And that's when I realized what I was looking at . . .

'No way!' I gasped.

Holding the can of paint was me! ME! *My* beanie, *my* puffer jacket, *my* rubbish fake Nikes that Dad had bought off Market Abdul for a tenner. Only it wasn't me! I had never done that!

'That ain't me!' I yelled. 'I've never seen that graffiti in my life.'

The policeman didn't even bother arguing. He just turned to the next photo. The guy who looked like me had finished his spray-painting and had taken a step back to admire his work. I could see more of his face now and the likeness was incredible. He was my spitting image! My clone! And right there in front of him, written on the wall in big letters, were the words:

'I know that wall,' I mumbled, sounding dazed. 'That's the back of the canteen.'

'Don't play dumb,' said the policeman. 'Course you know where it is. You wrote it.'

'I didn't!' I cried. 'Why would I tag up the school a month after I saved it from –' I paused, not just because I remembered that I wasn't allowed to tell anyone about the aliens, but because the policeman had flipped to the final photo. The picture showed another kid painting an exclamation mark at the end of 'SCHOOL SUCKS!' And then I realized who it was – Umer! Or at least some guy who looked exactly like him.

'But . . . I . . . we . . . it wasn't . . . we didn't . . .' was all I could manage to say.

'Don't even try it, boy!' growled my father. 'You

can't talk your way out of this one!'

He had a point. What could I possibly say? There was photographic evidence. Only, it wasn't me. I'd never been so sure of anything in my life.

'It's a set-up,' I said lamely. 'I've been framed.'

'THAT IS IT! THAT IS THE LAST STRAW!' yelled my dad so loudly that the ugly ornaments on the windowsill rattled.

'Mohammed!' said my mum, appearing out of nowhere.

'Aargh!' I yelled, jumping back. How does she do that? I swear she wasn't in the room before. I think she must dress to match her surroundings. She's like some big Asian chameleon, blending into the room. That afternoon she had on her swirly purple shalwar kameez, which is exactly as ugly as our wallpaper (and, trust me, that's some seriously ugly wallpaper – it looks like a puke ate puke and puked).

'Do not shout in front of the policeman,' continued my mum, not showing a hint of emotion.

'I will shout in front of whoever I like!' shouted my dad.

That was true. I once saw him get kicked out

of a funeral after he heard Pakistan had lost the cricket. If Dad wanted to shout, he was gonna shout. And it was shouting time.

'I will punish you so badly, Humza, you will never forget it!' yelled my dad. 'I will punish you so badly they will turn it into a movie about punishments and show it to other idiot children as a punishment! I will punish you so badly –'

And this just kept on going. He was off on one now and there was no saying when he'd come back down. The police officer was starting to look a bit nervous – probably wondering if he'd end up with a murder on his hands. (A Humzacide!)

Sadly, I knew Dad would never actually go so far as to kill me. There was too much sport to be had in torturing me for years. And I reckon he'd have kept on ranting forever if the doorbell hadn't rung and interrupted him. I didn't care who it was. Any distraction was welcome.

Or so I thought. It turned out to be exactly the opposite of what I needed. When my mum returned from the front door, she was accompanied by another policeman. And he wasn't alone. Behind him stood my best friend and his disappointed-looking parents.

Umer's mum and dad were just as short and round as him. Standing together in a huddle, they kinda looked like those little space bears from Star Wars. But not the happy dancing kind that just blew up the Death Star. These were three miserable-looking Ewoks.

'Can I come and live with you?' whispered Umer as he joined me.

'I was gonna ask you the same thing,' I replied.

'Maria, Hassan,' said my mum to Umer's parents, 'please, take a seat while we figure all this out.'

What followed was an hour of being shouted at from all sides. It didn't take long for the two coppers to realize that there was no point in them pitching in. Whatever punishment the law could dish out, it couldn't compete with the creative fury of four angry Asian parents.

'Good luck, boys,' said one of the policemen as they headed for the door. 'Looks like you're gonna need it.'

When Dad came back from showing them out, he was carrying something that would change my life forever.

'Ha!' shouted Dad. 'I have it! And to think that someone posted it right through the door, just when we needed it most!'

He was holding a piece of paper and waving it about in the air. He actually looked kind of happy. That was a bad sign.

'What are you talking about, Mohammed?' said my mum.

'The punishment!' he said with an enormous grin. 'I have it! *This* is the answer to all of our discipline problems! With this piece of paper, we shall at last fix our useless, dull-witted, out-of-shape sons!'

'Who you calling useless and dull-witted?' I yelled. (I figured I'd let him have out-of-shape.)

'Shut up, boy!' said my father. 'Your days of backchat and mischief are over! This place is the answer!'

'What place? Tell us!' asked Umer's dad, getting caught up in the excitement.

'Here!' my dad replied, holding out the flyer for everyone to see.

It showed a picture of some grumpy old bald guy, standing in front of a group of unhappy-looking kids. Above that were the words THE MAHMOOD ACADEMY – SUMMER SCHOOL PROGRAMME.

'Summer school?' I yelled. 'You've got to be kidding me! Those two words should never go together!'

'*Oooh*,' said Umer's mum. 'That sounds like a very interesting option.'

It didn't. It sounded like a terrible idea. Maybe the worst idea since Dad gave me the hand-me-down Y-fronts my cousins had grown out of. (No man should ever have to wear another man's pants – that's just a fact.) But there was something about the flyer that was disturbing me even more than the words 'summer school'.

'Er . . . that don't look like Eggington,' I said, feeling very nervous all of a sudden.

'It is not!' said my dad triumphantly. 'It is Pakistan! Very close to where I grew up!'

'Pakistan!' Umer and I cried at the same time. There was no way I was going to spend my summer in Pakistan. Especially not at some school!

Thankfully, I could always rely on my mum to step in at the last minute and save the day. She had my back. Thank God for Mum.

'I think it is a sensible idea,' said Mum.

'What?' I cried. 'You're meant to be the one who stops this madness!'

'You have crossed a line with this behaviour, Humza,' she continued. 'It is too much, too often.'

'It's a stitch-up, I swear! We didn't do it!'

'Your father's right. You really do need some discipline,' said Mum, sounding more sad than angry. 'I cannot help you any longer if you won't help yourself.'

'But I can't go to Pakistan!' I protested. 'I've got important things going on! Big plans!'

'Ha!' scoffed my dad. 'Like vandalism? Like disturbing the peace? You have never done an important thing in your life!'

Aarghhh! Man, I was desperate to tell him about the alien invasion. I couldn't believe he didn't remember a thing! He'd been proud of me that day. For ten minutes, he'd been properly proud of me. But now it was gone and I was back to getting punished unfairly again.

'Then it is agreed,' said my father. 'Our idiot sons are going to Pakistan!'

And, I swear, I could almost hear the flushing sound as all my plans for the summer vanished down the toilet.

CHAPTER THREE
PAKISTUNNED

When we caught up with Wendy in the park the next morning, she couldn't believe it either.

'What do you mean, "Pakistan"?' she asked, sounding confused.

'It's a place in Asia,' I replied. 'It's where they make Pakistanis.'

'I know where it is,' said Wendy. 'But why are you two going there?'

'Our parents have enrolled us at summer school,' said Umer. 'It's a punishment.'

'A punishment for what?' asked Wendy.

'That's the worst bit!' I barked. 'For something we didn't even do! They've got these photos of two kids with *our* faces spray-painting graffiti on the school. But I swear it ain't us!'

'It's true,' said Umer. 'We didn't do it.'

'You're saying you've been framed?' asked Wendy, sounding like she was struggling to believe it. 'By lookalikes?'

'Exactly!' I yelled. 'Someone's got it in for us. And when I find out who, I'm gonna make 'em pay.'

'There's something I don't understand,' said Wendy. 'Why are they sending you to Pakistan for this? You two are always getting in trouble. Why send you away now?'

'Bad timing,' I replied. 'Just as we were getting told off, my dad got a flyer through the letterbox for some Pakistani summer school. Normally Mum would stop him, but it turns out she was pretty angry too. Plus, she liked the sound of the place. Said it might finally stop me from being such an embarrassment to the family. Whatever that means.'

'My parents agreed,' added Umer. 'And now that they don't have to look after me all summer, they've decided to go to Disneyland by themselves. They're over the moon about it.'

'Wow . . .' said Wendy, shaking her head. 'I'm sorry, guys. That's pretty rough.'

'Tell me about it,' I replied. 'Pakistan's gonna be

like going back to the Stone Age.'

'Come on,' said Wendy. 'I don't think that's true. I bet it's a lot more modern than you imagine.'

'Trust me,' I replied. 'They probably ain't even got electricity, or cars, or Minecraft.'

'So you've never been before?' asked Wendy.

'I went as a baby,' I replied, 'but I don't really remember it. Probably blocked it out.'

'We've never been able to afford the trip,' said Umer. 'My parents were saving up for it, but when they got the chance to send me by myself, they couldn't resist.'

'When do you fly?' asked Wendy.

'Tomorrow,' said Umer.

'Really?' she replied. 'Wow, that's a bit quick.'

'We told you they were desperate to get rid of us,' I grumbled.

'Well, I guess we can always Skype?' suggested Wendy. 'That's how I'm going to talk to my parents while I'm at camp.'

'Yeah, right,' I replied. 'There ain't gonna be no Wi-Fi in Pakistan. There probably won't even be toilets. Plus, even if we could get online somewhere, how are we meant to Skype? Umer's phone's older than Stonehenge, and all I've got is a stupid pager.'

'Um, maybe we could send postcards?' suggested Wendy.

'Great, more writing,' I muttered. 'Just what I want to do while I'm at school.'

Everyone was quiet after that. I felt a bit bad for being so negative, but so would you be if you had to spend your whole summer at school in a foreign country. And, yeah, I know I'm Pakistani and all, but I ain't *from* Pakistan. It's as foreign to me as it would be to anyone else who grew up in the UK. Home for me is Poundland, and Argos and KFC (the halal ones at least). What the hell was I gonna do in Pakistan?

Thankfully, Grandpa was always pretty good to talk to when I was worried about something. He was as wise as he was old-looking. He had white scruffy hair, a big bald spot and more wrinkles than Umer's shaved cat. Unfortunately, when I walked into his place, it looked like he might already have enough on his plate without my problems as well.

'Damn, Grandpa, what is all this mess?' I asked, looking around the bomb site that used to be his living room.

'Packing,' replied Grandpa with a grim nod

as he surveyed the battlefield of discarded shoes, sunglasses and sun cream. There were suitcases open all over the room, spilling out clothing of every description.

'Oh yeah, Peru,' I said, remembering his holiday plans.

Having nearly lost Auntie Uzma to those alien slugs, Grandpa had decided it was time he started taking better care of her. I think he felt kinda guilty about how much of his life he had devoted to working at the Agency. And, because Auntie Uzma had always dreamt of going on a big holiday to South America, Grandpa made that his top priority.

'Do you really need this much stuff?' I asked him.

'No,' replied Grandpa. '*That* is my case.' He pointed to a small, battered leather suitcase in the corner of the room.

'Oh. So then all *this* is . . .'

'Auntie Uzma's.' Grandpa sighed.

'Whoa . . . she means business . . .'

'I certainly do!' came Auntie Uzma's cry as she marched into the room carrying a dozen dresses and a stack of sun hats. 'This is our first holiday in fifteen years and we are doing it right!'

'Sure. But how many pairs of flip-flops do you really need, Auntie?' I asked, picking up one of the dozen or so sandals that were lying in a heap by the telly.

'Seven!' snapped Auntie Uzma. 'Possibly eight!'

She threw the big pile of clothes on to the only bit of sofa that wasn't already covered in packing. It was, however, being occupied by a sleeping cat named David Chesterton.

And if you're wondering how a cat ends up with such a stupid name, it's cos my auntie and uncle inherited him from their dead neighbour, who was also named David Chesterton. Turns out they'd never thought to ask the guy what his cat was called before he popped his clogs. So when the mourning moggie moved in with them, they just borrowed the dead guy's name. I mean, it's not like he was using it any more.

So that's why there was a scruffy old furball, called David Chesterton, asleep on my auntie's sofa when she dumped half a wardrobe on his head. He barely had a chance to open his eyes before being buried in an avalanche of dresses.

'*Meeeooooww*,' said the pile of dresses unhappily. A moment later, David Chesterton's head popped up through the middle of the heap, right into a big yellow sun hat. It kinda suited him.

'*Purrrp*,' he said when he saw me – and for just a second I thought he might be smiling. (Damn it . . . cats can smile! I hate it when my dad's right about stuff.)

'Right! Move these things,' said Auntie Uzma, sweeping all the photos and trinkets that were on the mantelpiece into a nearby armchair. She began laying out a parade of different sunblocks along the ledge, where the decorations had been.

I bent down and picked up one of the pictures that had crashed on to the seat. It was an old black-and-white shot of a couple of kids in a marketplace. One was tall and smiling, and the other was short and grumpy.

'Hey, is that my dad?' I asked, pointing to the scruffy little boy with the big frown.

'It is,' said Grandpa, grinning. 'He was angry that day because I beat him in a race. But, to be fair, I was twice his size.'

'Wait, that's not . . . It is!' I cried, recognizing the tall boy. 'That's you! I can't believe it! You look so young!'

'I was fifteen,' he replied. 'Pretty fresh, yes?'

'Yeah, man,' I said, laughing. 'I had no idea you ever looked like a kid. Is that Pakistan?'

'That's right. The market in our village. Here,' he said, slipping the photo from its frame, 'why don't you keep it? To know where you come from.'

'I can't take this,' I told him.

'I'm sure I have another,' he replied, handing it to me. 'I insist.'

'Thanks, Grandpa,' I said, accepting the picture. 'Actually, Pakistan's kinda what I came to talk to you about. Have you got time for a chat?'

Grandpa looked over to where Auntie Uzma was forcing an entire women's fashion department into a suitcase with her mighty arms.

'Definitely,' he replied. 'I need some air.'

Ten minutes later, we were sitting at the ice-cream parlour, sharing a massive banana split.

'And now they're planning on sending me to summer school against my will,' I told Grandpa, stabbing my spoon into the banana to emphasize my point.

'It is not forever,' said Grandpa with a kind smile, all gappy teeth and gums.

'That ain't the point. It isn't fair. I didn't do anything wrong this time. It's a set-up.'

'It sounds like no one's going to believe you,' he said, taking a bite of ice cream.

'Yeah, no one but you,' I replied, shaking my head. 'I wish we could just tell them about the space slugs, then they'd treat me with some respect.'

'You did a very brave thing when you fought off those aliens,' said Grandpa. 'But perhaps the hardest part will be living with the fact that no one can ever know.'

'Yeah. Still seems a bit over the top though. Did they really have to wipe *everyone's* memory?'

'There would be panic if word got out about alien invaders,' replied Grandpa with a frown so wrinkly you could lose spare change in the folds. 'The Agency are just trying to keep the peace.'

'Fine, but why haven't they contacted me yet? I've held up my end of the bargain. I ain't told no one.'

'It will happen in time,' replied Grandpa. 'Be patient.'

'I've been patient! Now I'm ready to do some spying. I want my gadgets! I want a bike that fires missiles or a skateboard that turns into a jet.'

'I'm not sure those have been invented yet,' he said with a grin.

'Well, it doesn't matter now. I'm probably going to miss out on the whole opportunity. They'll ring me the minute I get shipped off to summer school and it'll be too late. What a mess.'

We were both silent for a time. I stared out of the window at a pigeon who was trying to impress another pigeon with his puffed-out chest. Stupid pigeons.

'Look on the bright side,' said Grandpa eventually. 'At least you don't have a hole in your hand.'

'Huh?' I replied, looking up at him.

He was holding a coin between his finger and thumb and smiling at me.

'If you had a hole in your hand like I do,' he continued, 'you would lose money all the time, see?'

And, as he said it, he tapped the coin on the back of his other hand, once, twice, three times. On the third tap, the coin fell right through his skin and on to the counter in front of us!

'Whoa!' I gasped. 'How'd you do that?'

'I was going to save this until I was back from Peru, but perhaps today is the day I teach you your second magic trick.'

'Really?' I said, sitting up in my seat. 'I promise I'll practise every day. I won't tell anyone else how it's done.'

'I know, Humza,' he said with a wrinkly grin. 'You are a natural magician. Now, do you still have the coin I gave you?'

'Of course I do!' I replied, slipping Grandpa's antique coin from my pocket. 'I carry it everywhere.'

'Excellent.' He smiled. 'Then do exactly as I do.'

CHAPTER FOUR
THE BIG DAY

Before you could say 'Please don't send me to Pakistan', the big day arrived. And by 'big' I mean 'awful', and by 'arrived' I mean 'smashed into my life like a cricket ball in the head'.

I was sitting in the back of the car between Grandpa and Auntie Uzma, who were hitching a lift with us to the airport. Turns out their flight was leaving just an hour after ours. Mum was up front next to Dad, who was driving like he didn't even have a brake pedal.

'Out of my way, stupid idiot!' shouted Dad, swerving round a little old lady who he'd cut up on the inside lane. 'We have a plane to catch!'

'Two planes!' corrected Auntie Uzma with an

excited giggle.

Umer was due to meet us at the terminal in half an hour with his parents. Unfortunately, we wouldn't be flying alone. We had a chaperone joining us. Yup, Dad was coming along to make sure we got there OK. Or, rather, to make sure we didn't parachute out of the plane and start a new life on a tropical island somewhere.

'Grandpa,' I said quietly, when there was a good moment. 'There must be some way you can get me out of this? Can't you talk to the Agency? See if they can pull some strings and get this whole summer school shut down or something?'

'You never know, Humza,' he replied with a warm smile. 'You may enjoy your time in Pakistan more than you think.'

'But I'm not meant to be there! I'm meant to be here, training as a spy! The Agency are gonna be fumin' when they find out I'm not around. How are they gonna contact me now?'

'Maybe this will help,' said Grandpa, reaching into his hand luggage. 'I have a gift for you.'

'A gift?'

'We'll call it a late birthday present,' he said, smiling as he slipped a wrapped parcel from his bag.

'But Auntie Uzma already gave me a hoodie.'

'Hoodie is fine. But you are twelve now. Isn't it about time you had your own mobile telephone?'

OH. MY. GOD.

My own phone! Finally! I'd been waiting years for this! I began ripping open the parcel as fast as I could. I was going to download every game possible before we got on that flight. I was going to use every penny I had in my savings to get shows and movies and music. This was going to save everything! This would get me through a month in Pakistan like nothing else could. OH . . . MY . . .

'*Huh?* What's this?' I said, lifting up the grey plastic brick that had tumbled out of the package.

It was HUGE. You'd have had trouble fitting it into a can of Pringles. The charger alone was bigger than most phones. The handset had these chunky rubber buttons, a stubby little antenna and a tiny green display. And, man, was it ugly! 'Ugly' doesn't even do it justice. If the winner of the Ugliest Dog in the World competition had spent its prize money having its bum glued to its face, it still wouldn't have been half as ugly as this phone. It was a mess.

'It's your new telephone,' said Grandpa cheerfully. 'Good model. Never break down.'

'*New* telephone?' I replied, unable to believe what I was looking at. 'It looks Victorian. Where do I put the coal?'

'Ha.' Grandpa laughed. 'Now you can stay in touch with us from anywhere in the world.'

'You're saying this is gonna work in Pakistan?'

'Oh yes, that's where I got it,' replied Grandpa.

'I should have guessed,' I said, doing my best to hide my frustration. 'Thanks, Grandpa. I appreciate it.'

And I did. I mean, obviously, it was the worst phone I'd ever seen, but I could see he meant well.

And it *was* kind of him. I just hoped it wouldn't blow our luggage allowance because it weighed more than the Great Wall of China.

Man, what's a kid got to do to get a smartphone around here?

At the airport, the mums cried and the dads shouted – so nothing new there. Umer's suitcase failed check-in because of all the food his mum had stashed inside it for the trip. The woman at the desk said they'd have to reduce the weight before she'd let it through, so for the next ten minutes Umer and his parents stood there stuffing pakora and samosas into their mouths. Eventually, when the people in the queue behind us looked like they might start rioting, the woman checked them through. We hadn't even left the airport yet and already an entire planeload of Pakistanis wanted to kill us. It was a great start.

I hugged my mum goodbye at security and promised her I'd be good. Right up until the last minute, I was hoping she'd change her mind and stop me going.

'Come on, Mum,' I begged. 'You're meant to be the one who rescues me from this stuff.'

She still looked a little tearful as she smiled at me. 'You are a good boy, Humza,' she said. 'I *know* you are. You are just a magnet for trouble. Be safe out there. Make me proud. And learn some Urdu, for crying out loud! You are twelve! It's embarrassing!'

She gave me one last big squeeze, as hard as she could, then hurried away sobbing. I couldn't believe it. What did *she* have to cry about? I was the one getting shipped off to the Middle Ages!

When all the goodbyes were done and the security men were giving us evils for holding up the line, we followed Dad through to departures.

'Grandpa, man, is there no way you can get me out of this?' I begged as we arrived at our gate. 'You're my last hope!'

'Humza,' he replied, kneeling down and looking me in the eye. 'You are going to Pakistan. Trust me, it's about time.'

And, with that, he gave me a hug, then headed off with Auntie Uzma, dragging behind them the biggest pile of luggage anyone has ever taken on a two-week holiday.

'BYE-EEEEEEE!' shrieked Auntie Uzma over her shoulder, waving like a circus seal. I hadn't seen her so excited since the all-you-can-eat buffet came to House of Raj.

I'd have felt happier for them if I hadn't been so miserable about my own trip.

'You never know,' said Umer, who'd noticed the look on my face. 'Maybe it'll turn out all right.'

'You mean the plane might crash?' I replied.

'Very funny,' he said with a grin as he put his arm round my shoulder.

'Come on, slow boys!' shouted my dad, ignoring the queue of passengers waiting in an orderly line and making his way right up to the gate.

'There's a queue, sir,' said the flight attendant who was collecting the tickets.

'Yes,' agreed my dad, glancing behind him. 'And I am at the front of it.'

She stared at him for a time, weighing up if he was worth the trouble, then snatched our tickets and checked us through.

As I stepped from the solid floor of the airport terminal into the hollow neon tube of the boarding bridge, I had a sudden sinking feeling. We hadn't even taken off yet and already my bedroom in Eggington felt very far away.

Pakistan, here we come . . .

★

Hot. Oh my God. So hot! Actually, 'hot' doesn't even do it justice. Boiling, scorching, blistering – there ain't a word in the English language to cover that kind of heat. It was like skinny-dipping in a vindaloo. And that was just the runway. Just the short sprint between the door of the plane and the air-conditioned terminal. It can't have taken more than forty-five seconds. How was I ever gonna adjust to this?

'Idiot boy!' shouted my dad. 'Take off your hat and coat. This is not England.'

The coat seemed like a good start. But the hat never comes off. Never.

The inside of the airport was a bit of a surprise. I ain't prejudiced or nothing, but I just assumed there'd be more goats and chickens and stuff. Maybe a dirt floor, and fights breaking out here and there. Funny thing is, it looked pretty much like the airport in England – passport counters, luggage collection, all of it.

'Did we definitely get on the right plane?' I asked my dad while we waited for our bags. 'This doesn't look like Pakistan.'

'What? Stop talking nonsense!' he replied, ignoring my legitimate concern.

If it was the wrong place, it was definitely popular with Pakistanis. They were everywhere. It was like Birmingham.

'They got some OK shops here,' I said to Umer. 'Check out those phones.' I pointed to a nearby electronics shop selling dozens of different smartphones. Proper brands too. It was weird, cos I'd just expected to see more big ugly bricks like the one Grandpa had given me. Man, I still couldn't believe I had that thing in my hand luggage . . .

Next to the phone shop was a place selling clothes, stuff I'd actually consider wearing. And beside that was a . . . *No way!* A KFC!

'Whoa,' said Umer. 'Fried chicken. Maybe it won't be as bad as you thought.'

'Hmm, I don't know,' I replied. 'It's probably just the airport that's like this. I bet it's gonna be horse-and-cart rides from here on out . . .'

Turns out the taxi we got in was a proper car, with petrol, wheels and – best of all – air conditioning. After having spent another thirty seconds in the scorching heat, it felt like heaven. I hoped I'd never have to get out. Looking around the car, I reckoned it was probably nicer than my dad's one back home.

Though, to be fair, my dad does have a pretty lame car. Sometimes I think the only thing holding it together is the dirt.

'Welcome to Pakistan, boys!' said Dad, craning his neck round from the front seat to look at us, a big grin on his face. 'What do you think?'

'Hot!' I yelled.

'Ha.' My dad laughed. 'Yes! A wonderful heat. Boils the blood!'

Was that meant to be a good thing? It didn't sound like a good thing. Looking out the window, I saw loads of tall buildings everywhere, big towering things whizzing past us along the motorway. We passed houses, shopping malls, a sports stadium . . . and everyone I saw had a better mobile phone than mine. I guessed maybe they did have electricity and toilets here after all. Maybe I'd been a bit quick to judge. This was a proper city after all. Of course, it wasn't all tall buildings and shopping malls. Pakistan ain't a rich place, and a lot of people we saw out of the window looked like they were working hard for not very much.

One thing I will say, though, is that I finally got to learn why my dad drives like he does. I'd never heard so much beeping in my life. Every car was at it constantly. It's not like in England where you just beep to tell someone they've annoyed you. In Pakistan, they were doing it every few seconds, just to let people know they were there and about to do something dangerous. Seriously, there were cars driving down the wrong side of the road, going up on the pavement, nudging each other out of the way. It was wild. And the noise never let up.

Umer and I held on tight in the back as we skidded round a corner, braking hard to avoid running into entire families on a single moped. My dad didn't seem worried though. He was so relaxed that he fell asleep twice.

At one point, we stopped at a set of traffic lights, and I noticed a kid sitting nearby on the kerb. His clothes were a bit ragged and his hands and face were grubby with dust. Slumped beside him was a big bag of plastic bottles. I figured he must have been gathering them up off the street.

As I watched him, he suddenly turned and looked up at me. We stared at one another for a moment. I lifted my hand and gave him a little wave. He waved back. Then the lights changed and we drove away.

Eventually, we skidded to a stop outside an

enormous train station. Through the fence, I could see hundreds of people piling on to a train. Literally on top of it! Sitting on the roof and everything!

'Ah, we are here!' said my dad.

'Here?' I asked. 'The train station? You mean, we're not staying in the city?'

'What? Of course not!' he barked. 'Why would we stay here?'

'Cos it seems all right. I could spend a month here. You know, if I had to.'

'Ha! You think we come to Pakistan to stay in the city? No chance! You are here to see the real Pakistan!'

And, before I knew it, we were sitting inside a long green train with 2,000 other people, heading out into the middle of nowhere.

CHAPTER FIVE
SUMMER SCHOOL

After what felt like forever, we arrived at our stop. I'd spent most of the day practising Grandpa's magic trick, because there wasn't much else to do on the train. I was concentrating so hard that I didn't even realize we'd got to our station until my dad nudged me.

'You see that village?' he said, pointing out of the window to a little town, far in the distance.

'Yeah,' I replied. 'Is that where we're going?'

'No. It is where I was born.'

'Whoa,' I said, smiling up at him. 'You've travelled a long way, Abu-jee.'

Sometimes, when I forget that Dad and I don't get along that well, I call him Abu-jee, like I used to when I was little. It just means 'Dad', but I think he likes it. I think we both kinda do.

I stared down at the tiny town my dad had come from. There were dozens of small sand-coloured buildings scattered between a winding river and the shadowy edge of a forest. At the centre was a small mosque, with its crescent-moon minaret sticking out the top. Beside it was what looked like a little market square.

'Hey!' I said, suddenly remembering what I'd stuffed into the bottom of my hand luggage. 'Is that where this was taken?' I slipped the black-and-white photo from my bag, the one of him and Grandpa as kids.

'Ha!' Dad laughed when he saw it. 'Where did you get this?'

'Grandpa,' I told him. 'He said he beat you in a race that day.'

'Nonsense!' snapped my dad. 'He cheated! It is not my fault he was born six years too early!'

'Can we go down there?' I asked him. 'To your village?'

'No time,' he replied. 'We have to get you to the school. I will go there after I've dropped you off.'

'But I'd like to see where you grew up,' I told

him – and I meant it.

'Perhaps when I collect you,' he said, putting his hand on my shoulder. 'If there is time. Now come on, we had better get off before this thing starts moving again.'

As Dad jumped up to get our luggage, Umer leaned over to me. 'Is that really your uncle?' he asked, pointing to the picture. 'I can't believe he used to be a kid.'

'I know, right,' I replied, grinning. 'Full head of hair and everything.' We were both laughing as we grabbed our bags and headed off the train.

It didn't last. The heat outside was even worse than it had been in the city. You could see it in the air. It made the train tracks shimmer and wobble on the horizon, like when you look through fire. The concrete platform was hot enough to melt your shoes if you stood still for too long.

I was already sweating.

Umer looked like he might die.

'I think I might die,' groaned Umer.

'You won't die,' I told him, handing him my water. 'You ain't allowed to die. Cos that'd mean I'd be stuck here by myself, and that ain't happening.'

'*Nnughh*,' he replied, gulping down a mouthful

of water and handing the bottle back.

Dad was already talking to the station guard in Urdu, but I didn't have a clue what he was saying. The guard nodded, then turned and walked back to his office.

'Excellent,' said Dad, slapping his hands together. 'We have a chingchi coming.'

'What the hell's a chingchi?' I said.

'Chand gari,' said Dad to clarify, but Umer and I just stared at him. 'You know, a moon car? A motorcycle rickshaw? Don't you know anything?'

'Like a taxi?' said Umer.

'Yes, like a taxi.' Dad sighed, shaking his head.

Yeah, right. When the chingchi turned up, it didn't look like any taxi I'd ever seen. Seriously, it barely resembled a car. It was more like someone had jammed a motorbike halfway into a shed, then painted the whole lot to look like a clown's nightmare. It was covered in flashing neon lights, like a Christmas tree, and inside there were a load of trinkets and other random junk stuck all over the dashboard. It was fifty per cent wood, fifty per cent metal, and one hundred per cent ugly.

But I gotta tell you, it was fun. It was like Mario Kart on one of the super-bumpy dirt levels. The

ground was so rough, riding on it felt like being in an earthquake. Umer kept trying to speak but all that came out was '*M-n-n . . . g-g-g . . . t-t-t . . .*' I had no idea what he was saying so I just laughed and nodded. Dad was crammed into the cab with us and it was a tight squeeze.

The driver had wedged all our luggage on to the roof and it was so tall we kept whacking tree branches down as we flew past. He was sitting up front on his motorbike seat, bouncing around like some rodeo guy. He kept looking round and smiling, with these bright red teeth, stained from whatever he'd been chewing. I couldn't help smiling back.

It turned out I was having fun after all. I hadn't

expected that. It was just a pity that, at the end of the road, there was a school waiting for us . . .

Ten minutes later, we arrived in a cloud of dust. When the haze cleared and I wasn't coughing any more, I saw we'd stopped outside the building from the summer-school flyer. A sign by the gate confirmed: The Mahmood Academy Summer School. It was a pretty big place, considering it was out here in the middle of nowhere. Weird location for a school.

The building was only one storey tall, but it was wide. It just kept going and going. The outside was a dusty white colour, with thick red columns every now and then. The windows were dark and I couldn't see a thing going on inside.

Before Umer and I had even got out of the rickshaw, the front doors to the building burst open and a little bald guy walked out. It was the guy from the flyer. He wore a smile as tight as a clenched fist and a three-piece suit so rigid it was a miracle he could even walk in it. On his face was the most perfectly carved beard I'd ever seen. It was like every last hair was terrified of being even slightly out of place.

But it was his bald head that was most impressive. He must have waxed it to get that shine. It looked like Auntie Uzma's dining table. He strode over to us as Dad was stepping out of the cab and snatched him by the hand. Dad stumbled towards him, pulled off balance by the force of the handshake. The man tugged Dad this way and that, squeezing Dad's palm until his knuckles clicked.

'Holy hell, man!' said my dad, snatching his hand back. 'What kind of handshake is that?'

'Ha!' said the bald man. 'Same old Mohammed Khan. Soft!'

'What?' replied Dad, confused. 'Do I know you?'

'Oh, so even your brain is soft now?' replied the man. 'You have spent too long in the Great Britain.'

'Who *are* you?' said Dad, sounding irritated. 'Do you work here?'

'Work here?' said the man, starting to sound a bit annoyed himself. 'This is my school. I am principal. Headmaster! I own this facility.'

'Ah, good,' replied Dad. 'And how exactly do you know me?'

'Are you joking with me? We grew up in the same village!' said the man, gesturing vaguely into the forest.

'We knew each other as children?' asked my dad, looking unsure.

'Everyone knew my family!' barked the headmaster.

'Uh . . . Asif Butt?' said my dad.

'Asif Butt?' yelled the little man. 'The goat milker? No! I am not him! You think I am him?'

'I don't know,' said Dad. 'It's been thirty years.'

I could tell my dad had no idea who this guy was, and clearly old Baldy wasn't happy about it. He snarled and turned his attention to me and Umer, still sitting in the back of the cab.

'You boys, out!' he snapped. 'Now!'

Umer and I began to drag ourselves from the back of the rickshaw. What with the heat and the fact that our bones had turned into liquid from the ride, we weren't moving fast.

'I said NOW!' the man shouted. 'You think this is fun camp? You think this is clown time? This is school! You are here to work! You are here to do what I tell you, when I tell you! Now move!'

We moved faster after that. I was already hating summer school and I hadn't even got inside. My dad, on the other hand, seemed pretty happy with the result. He might not have had a clue who this angry bald guy was, but he seemed pleased we were already being shouted at.

'When you take them home in a month,' said the headmaster, 'they will be unrecognizable. Disciplined, fit, educated. Not the wretched meat sacks standing before us today.'

'Meat sacks?' said my dad, considering the insult for a time. 'Yes. Meat sacks! I like this name. Listen up, meat sacks, I am returning to the village. You are in good hands with . . .' He paused. He clearly still had no idea who this guy was. 'Er . . . with my good friend here.' Dad then turned to the headmaster and shook his hand again. This time, though, he was ready for it, and the two men tugged each other's arms back and forth, locking eyes. Neither would give the other one the satisfaction of knocking him off balance. This went on for about twelve seconds. They looked like idiots. Eventually, they let go of one another's hands and stumbled back a little.

'Abu-jee,' I said. 'Please! You can't leave us here. Let us come to the village with you instead. We'll learn loads just being there. I can see how you grew up.'

'Another time, Humza,' said my dad, looking down at me. 'Behave yourself while you are here. You too, Umer. This is not England.'

And, with that, he gave us each half a hug, then

into the rickshaw and shot off down the
A thin layer of dust settled on our pile of bags.
Umer and I turned and looked at the headmaster.
He must have only been three or four inches taller
than us, but the guy was tough. There was something boxy about him – like he was built out of
Lego. He had this big bulbous chest like Batman –
you know, if Batman had been a short Pakistani guy
dressed in tweed. And how was he not sweating in
a three-piece suit? I was only wearing a T-shirt and
shorts and I was dripping. I bet he had just shouted
at his armpits until they dried up. I could already
tell this was gonna suck worse than anything, ever.

'Pick up those cases and get inside,' snarled the
headmaster. 'You have lessons starting in three
minutes.'

'I was hoping to have a wash maybe?' I replied.
Normally I wouldn't care about stinking a bit, but
I'd been travelling since yesterday and I was sweating
worse than my dad eating a madras. I smelled like
something even the bin men wouldn't take.

Mainly, though, I was hoping that a shower
would buy me some time away from the bald
bull. I'd already spent the last twenty-four hours
in close proximity to one middle-aged Pakistani

maniac. I could do with a break.

'You will wash when you are told!' yelled the headmaster, stepping up so close that his wild eyes were only a centimetre from my own. 'You will eat when you are told, you will sleep when you are told, you will breathe when you are told!'

'Is now a good time to breathe?' I asked. Man, what was wrong with me? I knew as soon as the words had left my lips that they were a mistake.

'No,' he replied. 'In fact, if you take one more breath, you will sleep out here with the snakes.'

Huh? Was he serious? Was I not meant to breathe again? This guy was trying to murder me! Umer was looking nervous. At least he was allowed to breathe though. I had genuinely stopped inhaling because of this lunatic. I could feel my chest beginning to burn. The headmaster was just staring at me. He wasn't smiling, but there was a tiny glint of enjoyment in his eye. This guy was totally unhinged!

Just as my lungs were about to explode, he spoke. '*Now* you can breathe,' he said, then he turned to walk back into the school.

I gasped for breath, leaning over and putting my hands on my knees.

'Are you OK?' asked Umer.

I couldn't speak, but I nodded. There wasn't gonna be any getting round this guy. He was the enemy. And we were on his territory . . .

CHAPTER SIX
SCIENCE CLASS

The school was . . . well, a school. It could've been almost anywhere. Corridors, classrooms, students. Hundreds of students. Girls and boys. I could see them through the windows as we made our way down the hall, sitting at their desks, listening to their teachers. They were all sitting up super straight, and everyone was wearing uniform.

'Keep up!' snapped the headmaster, marching ahead of us.

'Man, I can't believe it,' I whispered to Umer. 'We've only been on summer holidays for a week and we're already back at school.'

'Yeah, and I bet we don't even get weekends,' Umer added, looking glum.

'Ah, what?' I cried, pulling my hat down over my

ears. 'I hadn't even thought of that!' Four straight weeks without ever leaving school. This must be what hell feels like.

The headmaster came to a stop outside one of the classrooms and peered in at the students with a look of suspicion. I don't know what he was so concerned about cos they all seemed pretty well behaved to me. When he was satisfied that a riot wasn't about to break out, he opened the door and walked in like he owned the place – which I guess he did.

'Mr Malik,' he said, interrupting the teacher at the front of the class, who jumped slightly as he turned to look at us. He was a doughy-looking guy with damp curly hair and half his shirt untucked. He had big round eyes that darted about the place like a lizard tracking a fly.

'Hmm . . .? Yes?' he replied with a smile.

'The new students have arrived,' said the headmaster. 'You boys! Here! Now!'

Umer and I stepped into the room, still clutching our cases. Every eyeball in the place turned to stare.

'Humza and Umer are from the United Kingdom,' said the headmaster, addressing the room.

'Despite this handicap, they will receive no special treatment. It is our job to toughen them up. Where they are soft, we will make them hard. Where they are weak, we will make them strong. When we are finished, they shall be unrecognizable!'

These kids must have spoken pretty good English to have understood all that. Which was a shame cos it was basically just a big insult.

'Right. Take a seat,' said Mr Malik, pointing to the back of the room. 'Hurry now. Time is wasting.'

Umer and I dragged our luggage to the end of the row and sat down at a pair of empty desks.

'And, um . . . yes . . . I'll be watching you,' said Mr Malik, glancing at the headmaster. 'No funny business . . . or . . . um . . . you will get the stick!' He grabbed a thin wooden rod from his desk and waggled it about.

The headmaster nodded his approval, then turned and left the room.

'I will not tolerate any . . .' began Mr Malik, then he paused and looked over towards the closed door. 'Is he gone?'

Some of the kids smiled and nodded.

'Phew,' he continued, turning to me and Umer. 'Welcome to the class, boys. And don't worry.

These days, we don't use the stick for punishments. Only experiments.'

And, with that, he lit one end of the wooden rod on a nearby Bunsen burner, then brought it beneath a green balloon suspended above the desk.

'Today, we are learning about hydrogen,' he added, with a grin.

There was a moment's silence before the balloon exploded in a huge fireball. Everyone gasped, then began to cheer.

Mr Malik put his fingers to his lips. 'Shh–shh–shh!' he said, smiling. 'We don't want to get in trouble this early in the day.'

'That was pretty cool!' said Umer.

'Yeah,' I agreed. 'I hope there's gonna be more explosions.'

'No smoke, see?' said Mr Malik, waving his hand through the air. 'Only steam. Very clean. Very powerful. Strong enough to push a rocket into space.' As he said this, he picked up a little toy rocket from his desk and threw it across the room. The girl at the desk beside Umer and me jumped up and caught it. The other kids laughed as she held up the rocket, grinning.

'In fact,' continued Mr Malik, 'the cloud created during a rocket launch is so immense that one hour later rain will pour down on a nearby farm. Rocket rain,' he added with a smile.

The kids all began to chatter at once, about the rocket rain and the explosion. Mr Malik didn't stop them. He just sat down at his desk and started preparing the next experiment.

'Hello,' said the girl who'd caught the rocket. She had a strong accent, a warm smile and a little gap between her two front teeth. Like most of the other girls at the school, she was wearing a thin green scarf over her hair, wrapped loosely round her neck and shoulders.

'Hey, how's it going?' I replied.

'Welcome to Pakistan,' she said. 'I am Azrah.'

'I'm Humza,' I said, 'and this is Umer.'

'Hi,' said Umer, leaning over me to shake hands.

'Are you from round here?' I asked.

'No,' replied Azrah. 'I am from near Lahore. My parents sent me here after I got in trouble.'

'Yeah, that's pretty much what happened to us,' I told her. 'What did you do wrong?'

'I took home a cat,' she replied.

'That doesn't sound too bad,' I said.

'And then another cat,' she added. 'And then another.'

'How many did you end up with?' I asked.

'Twenty-three,' she said with a little grin.

'Twenty-three!' I replied, laughing. 'Wow, you must really like cats!'

'I like *collecting* cats,' she said, and giggled.

'So what's there to do round here, with your time off?' asked Umer.

'Time off?' replied Azrah. 'We do not get time off. If we are not carrying out schoolwork, we

are doing physical exercise, chores or . . . well . . .
punishments. We get five hours to sleep, though, so
I try and enjoy my dreams.'

'Dreams?' I spluttered. 'I can't get by on dreams!
I need PS4! Television! Netflix!'

'I am afraid we do not have those things,' replied
Azrah. 'We have a goat you can milk though. That
is quite fun.'

'That just sounds like another chore,' I grumbled.

'Not if you pretend it is a cat,' said Azrah,
grinning.

'And why would anyone want to milk a cat?' I
asked.

'For cat milk,' replied Umer, like it was obvious.

Man, I could already tell this was going to be a
long month . . .

After that, the day only got worse. We were made to
go and change into our school uniforms between
lessons. They were these scratchy green trousers
and white shirts. I even had to wear a tie! Can you
believe that! Middle of the summer holidays and I
was wearing a tie! What kind of psycho makes you
dress up in stuff like that when it's forty degrees
outside! I was dying. This place was definitely the

worst punishment my parents had ever come up with. If I could even still call them parents, that is. I was beginning to think of them more as a pair of torturers who just happened to look like me.

Anyway, once we were dressed like idiots, it was time for maths class. And, I swear, it was taught by the hairiest man I'd ever seen. I thought he was a little bear when I first saw him. But bears can't be that boring. Seriously, it was like listening to paint dry. He had the world's most tedious voice. I had to keep poking myself in the leg with a pencil just to stay awake.

Next came PE, which in Pakistan must have stood for Pure Evil, cos it was the worst thing I'd ever gone through. The teacher was some former army guy named Sergeant Shah. He treated us like soldiers, making us run round the fields for miles in the heat while he shouted at us through a megaphone. And he never once got out of the little golf cart he rode around in. His massive pot belly was pressed up against the steering wheel so hard it kept beeping the horn every time he moved.

I tell you, I thought PE lessons at home were tough, but this was a hundred times worse. If anyone had thought to feed us so far, I'm pretty sure I'd have thrown up after about five minutes. Thankfully, though, we were starving, so I just dry-heaved a bit as we ran round the perimeter of the school again and again.

At one point, I stopped to catch my breath beside a dirty little shed at the edge of the fields. It turned out it belonged to Sunny, the school goat, who was even more unfriendly than he was smelly. He bit me almost immediately. Stupid goat.

After PE came geography, with some guy who'd clearly never heard of anywhere but Pakistan. Don't get me wrong, it was actually pretty interesting and I learned some stuff about Pakistan that my parents had never thought to mention. Like, everything. For example, did you know that Pakistan's bigger than the UK and France put together? And it's got the second-tallest mountain of anywhere on Earth. Plus, they've got this weird kind of blind dolphin that lives in the rivers and is nearly extinct. That's pretty cool, right? I mean, not if you're a blind dolphin, obviously – but I found it interesting.

I swear, this guy knew everything about Pakistan. He just didn't know a thing about the rest of the world. Someone asked him about Australia at one point and he acted like he'd never heard of it.

Seriously, I don't think he'd ever seen a world atlas before. Or, if he had, he hadn't liked it.

Throughout the day there were loads of breaks for Salah, which was fine by me cos I quite like prayer time, especially when life's hectic and you've got half a dozen teachers on your back. And finally there was dinner, which I'm pretty sure was served as a punishment. See, the one thing I *do* know about Pakistan is that we've got some of the best food in the world. Curries that would make you weep (and not just cos they're hot enough to strip paint off a postbox). I'm talking seriously tasty. But the stuff they were dishing out . . . urgh . . . They must have dug it up, hosed it down and left it out in the sun until it was warm enough to serve. It tasted like a hate crime.

Anyway, by the end of that first day, I knew I couldn't survive a whole month there. One way or another, I had to escape.

CHAPTER SEVEN
ESCAPE

'Escape?' hissed Umer, when we were in our beds that night. 'We can't escape!'

'*Shhh!*' I replied. 'Don't whisper so loud!'

We'd been given bunks next to each other in the boys' dorm and there were sleeping kids everywhere. I didn't want anyone waking up and hearing my escape plans.

It was a massive room with a long aisle running all the way down the middle. At the far end, there was a door leading to the toilets. There must have been a hundred other kids in with us, and they'd all passed out the moment the lights went off, exhausted by the day's exercises and punishments. But I was far too wired to sleep. I just wanted out of there.

'Where would we even go?' whispered Umer. 'We're in the middle of nowhere. We'd be eaten by snakes, or bears, or that scary headmaster.'

'We can go wherever we want, man! A couple of guys like us are gonna be treated like kings here. I bet we can become celebrities before the end of the week. I'll release an album, you'll get a talk show. It'll be sweet.'

'I'm not sure that's totally realistic, Humza.'

'Stop being so negative!' I snapped. 'Would you rather have your own talk show or die in a school?'

Umer thought quietly for a time.

'Are those the only options?' he said.

'Yes! And that's why you and me are getting out of here. Now! Tonight!'

'But it's dark.'

'Best time for an escape. Everyone's asleep.'

'Couldn't we just escape in the morning?'

'Why put off till tomorrow what you can do today?'

'I don't think that applies to getting eaten by wild animals,' objected Umer.

'Stop saying that! We'll almost definitely survive . . . I think.'

'Uh-uh. No way,' said Umer, and he rolled over

to face the other way. 'I'm not going.'

'Are you kidding me? You're actually gonna stay here?'

He didn't reply. I tell you, man, Umer can be stubborn, especially when you're putting his life at risk. I learned that when I tried to make him skateboard through a car wash.

'Fine,' I said, getting out of my bunk. 'I'll just go without you then.'

He rolled back over and stared at me for a moment. Then he smirked.

'You're not leaving,' he said. 'You're just going to the toilet.'

'Whatever,' I snapped, grabbing Grandpa's rubbish old phone from my bag. 'You'll miss me when you realize I've gone and I'm never coming back and you missed your chance to escape!'

'Uh-huh,' said Umer, rolling on to his other side.

Stupid Umer. He's known me too long – I *was* just going to the toilet. It's tough scamming someone you've been scamming since nappies. I wanted to stomp off in a huff, but the tiles were cold on my feet and it's pretty hard to storm anywhere on tiptoes. Instead I just crept away past row after row of sleeping students.

I clicked one of the big rubbery buttons on Grandpa's mobile and the tiny screen and keyboard lit up with a dull green light. It might not be any good as a phone, but at least it would work as a torch while I went for a wee. I could hear kids breathing all around me, dreaming about the endless schoolwork and punishments they'd get to enjoy in the morning. No thanks! I was getting out of there, even if I had to drag Umer with me. I just had to figure out how I'd convince him to come too. And there's no better place in the world to think than the toilet.

The dorms were in a separate part of the school grounds, across the exercise yard from the main building, where we had lessons. Thankfully, they had their own toilets, so I wouldn't need to go out into the night and get eaten by whatever it was Umer was so scared about. I used the glow from the phone to guide me out into the hallway and along to the little bathroom.

I closed the door behind me and turned on the light switch, scrunching my eyes up tight until they'd adjusted. Then I shut myself in one of the cubicles and sat down on the loo seat. I didn't really need a wee after all, but I definitely wasn't going back to bed straight away. It would serve Umer right if he thought I'd left without him.

I began to fiddle with the rubber buttons on the phone while I waited. And that was when I noticed the image on the screen. Right there, in the centre of the little green plastic rectangle, was a flashing envelope icon. *A message?* Who could have messaged me? No one knew my number. *I* didn't even know my number. It had to be Grandpa!

Just knowing that Grandpa might have been in touch started to make me feel better. I didn't have a clue how to open the app though. The phone looked nothing like a modern mobile: there was no touchscreen or fingerprint scanner, just the big rubbery buttons and the little green display. The ugly beige brick was as tall as my forearm, and deeper than it was wide.

I jabbed at a few of the buttons, but nothing happened. After a moment, I tried pressing the one labelled MENU. The envelope icon vanished. The screen went blank. Two letters appeared:

ID

What did that mean? I clicked the back button. Nothing happened. I pressed MENU again. Still nothing. I clicked OK. As soon as I did, the whole screen lit up. And not just a bit, either — it was blinding. This green laser exploded out of the phone, right into my eyes. I pulled my head back, but I still couldn't see a thing. I was about to drop the phone when the light stopped and the screen went dark again.

I blinked a few times to clear my vision. As my eyes adjusted once again to the light of the cubicle, I could make out the new text on the screen. It now read:

Identification confirmed: Agent Badman Continue?

Whoa . . . *Agent Badman* . . . Could this be what I thought it was? My finger hovered over the OK button . . .

The moment I pressed it, the phone came alive! Not just the screen, the entire phone! It split in two, right down the middle. The screen, the buttons, *everything* divided in half and began folding outwards. This time, the shock of it *did* make me drop the phone. It tumbled from my hands and on to the tiled floor with a crash. My heart was racing.

I pulled my feet up and watched over my knees as the phone kept unfolding, again and again, whirring and clicking and humming. Whole chunks of metal and plastic slid up and down, from one side to another, transforming and rearranging themselves into something new.

When it eventually came to a stop, the phone was no longer recognizable. This wasn't the ancient brick that Grandpa had given me a few days earlier. The device lying on the bathroom floor was like nothing I'd ever seen before.

A twelve-inch super-sharp full-colour screen sat at its centre, surrounded on all sides by a thin black frame. Built into the edges was a selection of buttons, lenses, ports, microphones, scanners, speakers and who knew what else. I had no idea what it was all meant to do, but I got the impression this device could do everything!

There was only one place it could have come from – the Agency! They must have had Grandpa give it to me. But why?

Before I could even start thinking it through, a line of text flashed up.

'What the . . .' I mumbled.

Then the text vanished and a familiar face appeared, floating in the centre of the screen.

'Hello, Agent Badman,' said Agent Akbar with a smile. 'Ready for your first mission?'

CHAPTER EIGHT
GADGET GUY

'What the what?' I gasped, staring at the face of
Agent Akbar looking up at me from the screen.
'Where are you calling me from? Are you still in
England?'

'I am not calling you at all,' replied the floating
head. 'I am only a digital representation of Agent
Akbar. A computer simulation.'

'Eh? What you on about?'

'I am a program, built into the operating system
of your communications device. An AI construct.'

'AI?' I mumbled.

'Artificially Intelligent software, based on the
personality of your Agency handler.'

'You ain't real?'

'I am real enough to help guide you on this

mission,' replied AI Akbar.

'*This* mission?' I asked, confused. 'Are you telling me it's already started?'

'It is no coincidence that you find yourself precisely where you are, Agent Badman.'

'On the toilet?'

'At the Mahmood Academy summer school,' replied AI Akbar. 'The Agency placed you there for a specific purpose.'

'Are you serious? You're the reason I'm out here? Why didn't you tell me?'

'I'm sure you have many questions,' said the simulation. 'But the information in my database is limited – I do not have the answers to everything. But I will do my best to tell you what I can and prepare you for the mission ahead.'

'All right, fine,' I replied. 'First up, who got me in trouble for that graffiti? That was you, right?'

'That information is classified,' said AI Akbar.

'I knew it!' I snapped. 'It *was* a set-up! How'd you do it? Who'd you hire to play me? Was it the Rock? I bet it was the Rock!'

'For the purposes of this mission, all you need to know is that an excuse was required for you to be sent here. A punishment from your parents proved the ideal cover.'

'So you framed me? Damn, man. That's pretty low.' I'd only been a secret agent for forty-five seconds and I was already fed up with how sly these spy organizations could be.

'As our youngest agent,' continued the simulation, 'you were the perfect candidate to infiltrate the summer school and observe the target.'

'Target? What target?'

'One of your teachers is not what he appears. He was once a member of our organization.'

'My teacher's an agent? No way! Which one? Is it Sergeant Shah? He used to be in the army apparently. Or is it the headmaster? He's definitely dodgy.'

'No, your target was never an agent,' replied the simulation. 'He was our head of research and development. He designed the items we use to arm and defend our agents in the field.'

'Oh, you mean your gadget guy,' I said.

'Gadget guy?' repeated AI Akbar.

'Yeah, like Q from James Bond. He made all the cool spy toys: laser watches and exploding pens and all that. All the sciency stuff –' And as soon as I said it, I knew. I was suddenly sure who the target was.

'Mr Malik!' I gasped. 'You want me to spy on my science teacher!'

'Indeed,' replied the simulation. 'Your mission is to discover whether he is still active in his research.'

'Why? What did he do wrong?'

'His work became dangerous,' replied AI Akbar. 'He was ordered to stop all experimentation until he could justify his research. When he refused, the Agency had no option but to cut off his resources and terminate his position.'

'You fired him for doing his own thing?'

'His research had the potential to wipe out every life form on the planet.'

'Oh,' I replied. 'I guess that is quite serious.'

'After his dismissal three years ago, he went into hiding. His whereabouts have only recently been discovered, here at the Mahmood Academy.'

'Yeah, teaching science. He's quite good at it, actually. Better than most of 'em. He does explosions.'

'Your mission, Agent Badman, is to investigate him. Discover whether he is continuing his research, or if he has truly changed his ways and moved on with his life.'

'And what if he hasn't?' I asked.

'Then he will be dealt with appropriately,' replied the little glowing head.

The following morning, Umer didn't seem entirely convinced of my sudden change of heart.

'So you've just decided to stay then?' he said, raising an eyebrow. 'You're not gonna run away after all?'

'Nope,' I replied, trying not to meet his eye. 'Just needed a good night's sleep. I'm feeling much better now.'

He was sitting on his bed giving me a hard stare, while all around us kids poured out of the dormitory towards the breakfast hall.

'You're telling me you've woken up and decided you like this place after all?' he asked.

'Uh-huh,' I replied with the most natural smile I could manage. 'Once you get used to the heat, and the work, and the exercise, it's actually got quite a cool vibe.'

'*A cool vibe?*' said Umer, clearly not believing a word of it.

'Well, maybe not a cool vibe, but . . . you know . . . I mean . . . we could learn something . . .' I suggested.

'You hate learning. Yesterday you said this place made you wish you had no eyes, ears or nose, so that if you had to be stuck here, at least you wouldn't know it.'

'Uh . . . yeah . . . well . . . that was probably just the jet lag talking.'

'What's going on, Humza?' he said, looking me dead in the eye. 'You're up to something.'

'Ah, man, please don't ask me. I'd tell you if I could.'

'If you *could*? What are you talking about? We never keep secrets from each other!'

'I promised. It's important. They made me.'

'They? Who's they?' said Umer. Then his eyes widened, his mouth fell open. 'The Agency!' he hissed.

'What? No! I don't know what you're on about!'

'I knew you were hiding something! I'm right, aren't I? It's them!'

'Ah, come on, man! I swore I wouldn't say.'

'I've been your best friend since you were born. I lent you my Nintendo when you broke your foot. I forgave you after you tricked me into shaving my cat. I've told you every secret I've ever had. You can't lie to me, Humza.'

Damn it. I had a responsibility to the Agency. A real one, like I'd never had before. But, truth is, I had a responsibility to Umer too. He was my best friend. Plus, he was only stuck out here because of me. I guess if I had to tell anyone in the world, at least I knew I could trust Umer.

'Fine, I'm gonna tell you,' I said, 'but you've got to promise to keep it top secret.'

Umer nodded but said nothing.

'OK,' I continued, 'so, after the whole alien thing, the Agency . . . they kind of asked me . . . if I wanted to be a secret agent.'

'THEY *WHAT*?' gasped Umer. 'Why didn't you tell me?'

'Oh, I don't know, it must have slipped my mind,' I said, rolling my eyes. 'Obviously I couldn't say anything! That's what being a secret agent means!'

'Well, how come they didn't ask me? I saved the world from aliens too.'

'I don't know. Probably just something to do with Grandpa. He must have vouched for me. I bet they'd have asked you otherwise.'

Umer went quiet for a bit. I felt terrible. First I'd let him down, and now I'd let the Agency down. I had to make the best of this. 'Hey, listen,' I said.

'If you want to, you can still be an agent for this mission.'

'What mission?' said Umer, lifting his head a little.

'This whole thing,' I replied. 'Turns out it's a mission. The Agency set it up. They're the ones who framed us and got us sent out here.'

'What!' cried Umer. 'You mean I could be at home playing FIFA?'

'Yeah, sure you could. You could be sleeping-in every day, watching the same old cartoons, eating your mum's weird daal. But ain't this more exciting?'

Umer stared at me but said nothing.

'The fact is,' I continued, 'they framed you too. So maybe they wanted you out here with me? Maybe they figured I might need your help? I bet they'd make you an agent too if you saved the day with me.'

Umer didn't seem convinced. He was giving me the look he always wore when I tried to persuade him of something. Man, that guy could be stubborn. He was harder to budge than my uncle Rabi when he falls asleep on the remote control.

'What do they want you to do?' Umer finally

asked, still sounding suspicious.

So I told him all about Mr Malik and how he'd been the Agency's gadget guy before he went missing. I explained how AI Akbar wanted us to watch him and find out if he was still up to anything.

'Well,' said Umer once he'd thought it through, 'I suppose if I'm stuck out here anyway . . .'

'Yes!' I yelled with a big grin. I went to put my arm round his shoulder, but Umer pulled away a little.

'No more secrets?' he added with a serious look.

'Deal,' I replied.

'OK then,' he said, his expression softening. 'Let's go do some spying.'

CHAPTER NINE
I SPY

Now that everything was out in the open and we had the dorm to ourselves, Umer and I were ready to begin our career as spies.

'Right, so how do we do it?' asked Umer.

'Do what?' I replied.

'Spying.'

'Oh . . . I think we just make it up as we go.'

'Didn't they give you any training?'

'Nope.'

'What about any gadgets?' asked Umer.

'Just Grandpa's mobile,' I replied, holding up the phone, which had switched back to its ugly brick mode.

'Oh . . .' said Umer, looking a bit lost. 'Well . . . in that case, what would James Bond do?'

'Hey, that's a great idea,' I replied. 'All right, so what's the first thing James Bond does when they give him a mission?'

'Fly off somewhere exotic?' suggested Umer.

'OK, good, we've done that bit. What next?'

'Hmm . . .' said Umer, thinking it through. 'Um . . . usually he just gets a girlfriend.'

'Oh. Right . . .' I replied.

'So, do you want to –'

'No!' I snapped. 'Don't even say it. In fact, forget James Bond. He's too easily distracted. What other spies are there?'

'Uh . . . what about that Mission Impossible guy?' suggested Umer.

'Oh yeah! With all the disguises! If we had disguises, we could go anywhere and no one would suspect a thing.'

'Great,' replied Umer. 'Let's go see what we can find!'

Half an hour later, Umer was standing by his bunk, wearing a mop on his head, a thick pair of reading glasses he'd found in a bin, and a bedsheet wrapped round him like a dress. 'How do I look?' he asked in his best impression of a girl's voice.

'Like a yeti,' I replied. 'What about me?'

'I'm not really sure what you're meant to be,' said Umer with a puzzled expression.

'I'm a statue, obviously!' I snapped.

'Is that toothpaste all over your face?'

'Yeah.'

'*My* toothpaste?' he asked, frowning.

'Well, I ain't gonna use mine, am I? I need it to brush my teeth.'

'I don't think you make a very convincing statue,' said Umer, sounding annoyed.

'Yeah, well, *you* don't look much like a girl.'

'I look *exactly* like a girl!' he yelled. Which was,

of course, the exact moment all the other kids decided to come back from breakfast. I spun round as the laughter hit me like a bus. All the boys from our dorm were standing near the door, cracking up. They were pointing at us and saying stuff I couldn't understand, bent over double in hysterics.

The laughter was so loud that other students, boys *and* girls, began to gather outside to see what was going on. I could see Azrah peering in through the window, grinning at us. I could feel myself starting to blush beneath the toothpaste.

'What is all this noise?' came a sudden bellow.

The laughter stopped in an instant. Every head turned as Mr Mahmood, the headmaster, barged through the crowd. I tried my best to wipe off my Colgate face mask with Umer's skirt but it was no good. Mr Mahmood had seen us. His eyes grew so wide I thought they might topple out of his big bald head.

'*Eeeennngliiiishhhhh boys!*' he growled through clenched teeth.

Oh well, so much for disguises.

The next thing I knew, I was on my hands and knees, cleaning a toilet with a toothbrush. Umer was in the neighbouring cubicle doing the same thing. Turns out Baldhead Mahmood hadn't taken kindly to us being out of uniform and making 'clown time' in his dormitory. Toilet-cleaning punishment was how he showed his displeasure.

'Damn it, man,' I said into the toilet bowl. 'We're missing science class!'

'How long before this thing's clean?' asked Umer, sounding miserable.

'It's never clean,' I replied. 'It's a toilet.'

'If we miss science, we'll have to wait until tomorrow to see Mr Malik,' said Umer.

'That can't happen,' I replied, straightening up. 'As you're my deputy agent, I think you should handle the toilet-cleaning part of the mission, while I take care of the spying bit.'

'Deputy agent?' said Umer, sticking his head under the wall that separated the two cubicles. 'Are you kidding?'

'Well, you ain't a real agent yet, so I figured I'd deputize you. And, obviously, if only one of us can go to the class, it should be the proper agent, right?'

'How are *you* a proper agent?' snapped Umer. 'No training, no gadgets. You didn't even make it all the way through the last Mission Impossible film.'

'That's only cos you got us kicked out of the cinema for eating too loudly!' I protested.

'Whatever. Just don't call me your deputy. And don't try to make me clean toilets for you. You said we could do this together. Equally.'

'I never *actually* said "equally".'

'Humza!'

'You know what?' I muttered, slamming my toilet lid shut. 'Forget this. These things are clean enough. You and me got more important business to take care of.'

'Well, at least we can agree on *that*,' said Umer, slamming down his own toilet seat.

We chucked our toothbrushes into the bin and sprinted off in the direction of science class.

When we skidded to a halt outside Mr Malik's room, I could see him through the glass, talking to the other students. It was weird seeing him again, now that we knew he might be some kind of evil genius. He still didn't look too evil though. He was smiling and waving his hands about as he spoke.

'Sorry we're late,' I said as I pushed open the door. 'We got in trouble.'

'Trouble, eh?' replied Mr Malik. 'Well, there are

worse things in life than a little trouble. After all, even from our gravest of errors, we may still learn a valuable lesson. Like Marie and Pierre Curie.' He gestured to the board, where he'd stuck up a couple of black-and-white pictures of whoever it was he was talking about.

'Were they forced to clean toilets too?' asked Umer.

'No, they died of radiation poisoning. But their discoveries changed the world.'

'Oh . . . well, if it's a choice between toilet duty and dying famous like those guys, I know which one I'd choose,' I replied.

'Take a seat,' he said with a smile. 'You too, Umer.'

How the hell was I meant to be suspicious of this guy when he kept being so nice? Couldn't he just be a big nasty idiot, like the headmaster? This was going to be harder than I'd thought.

We hurried to the back of the class and sat down beside Azrah.

'Good morning,' she said.

'Hey, Azrah,' I replied, avoiding eye contact. I was hoping she'd forgotten all about this morning's incident with the disguises. She seemed to be concentrating pretty hard on the lesson, so it looked like we'd got away with it.

'You have not missed much,' she whispered. 'Though that is mostly because everyone could not stop discussing your strange costumes. You looked very . . . interesting.'

Ah, man. I could feel myself starting to blush again as she grinned at me.

Umer gave me a nudge in the ribs. 'See, I told you,' he whispered, beaming. 'James Bond always starts by getting a girlfriend.'

'Shut up, Umer,' I said, and elbowed him back.

After I was done blushing, we turned our full attention to the mission. I don't think Umer and I had ever listened so hard to a teacher in our lives. Mr Malik was in the middle of telling everyone about the different chemical elements that made up everything in the universe. Next to the photos of those two dead scientists was a big colourful chart, labelled THE PERIODIC TABLE. Under normal circumstances, I'd have already been asleep. But I was so busy trying to work out if Mr Malik was evil or not that I accidentally started learning stuff. That had never happened to me before. Even now I can tell you that the melting point of lead is

327.5 degrees Celsius. What am I ever gonna do with that information?

No matter how hard we concentrated or how closely we watched him, Mr Malik never did anything evil the entire lesson. He just seemed like a science teacher. In fact, in that whole time, there was only one moment that felt strange. Just before the end, Baldhead Mahmood appeared at the door, staring through its little window with that suspicious/angry/bald look on his face.

'Oh, hello, Headmaster,' said Mr Malik as the headmaster strode into the room. 'Is there something we can help you with?'

'These two boys,' said the headmaster, pointing right at Umer and me. 'They have been disrupting your lesson? Making idiot games? Playing fool?'

'They've been very well behaved,' replied Mr Malik.

'Nonsense. These are bad boys. They need to be punished!'

'But they've done nothing wrong,' replied Mr Malik, frowning.

'They must have done something,' insisted Baldhead Mahmood. 'Have they been talking?'

'No,' said Mr Malik.

'Disrespectful?'

'Not at all.'

The headmaster was quiet for a moment. His gaze flicked between us and Mr Malik.

'And were they *late*?' he asked, his eyes thinning down until they were no more than evil little slits in his big cantaloupe head.

Ah, man! This guy was the worst. He *knew* we'd been late! *He* was the one who'd made us late in the first place. Mr Malik was silent for a moment. I could see he was stuck. If he said we'd been on time, the headmaster would catch him in a lie. But if he admitted that we'd arrived late, we'd get punished. And, for some reason, he didn't want that.

'After they had finished their punishment,' replied Mr Malik, 'the boys joined the class. They had not missed a great deal. But, to ensure they do not fall behind, I will be giving them additional work to complete.'

'Additional work?' said the headmaster, raising an eyebrow. 'Mmm, yes, good. Perhaps this will teach them not to be such useless khotas.'

'What's a khota?' I whispered to Umer.

'Donkey,' replied Azrah with a mischievous grin.

As the headmaster left the room, he had a big

smile on his face, clearly loving the fact we were going to be punished again so soon. When it was obvious that he wasn't coming back, the class began to chatter among themselves.

'Man, I hate that guy,' I said to Umer.

'I don't think you're the only one,' he replied, nodding towards the front of the room. 'Look.'

Mr Malik had an expression on his face I'd never seen before. His jaw was tight. His eye was twitching a little. It was subtle, but it was there. He was furious. Suddenly, the pencil he was holding snapped. And I don't just mean the tip – the whole thing! It cracked right in half. He'd been gripping it so tightly it had broken in two. (You ever tried to do that with one hand? It ain't easy.) And he didn't even seem to have noticed.

'Whoa,' I said. 'He does *not* look happy.'

'I don't think he likes being told what to do much,' said Umer.

'You're not kidding,' I replied.

And, as I said it, Mr Malik turned and looked straight at us. The moment he did, a smile burst across his face.

'Where was I?' he said. 'Ah yes, radium!' And then he went right back to speaking about chemicals until the bell rang. It was like a totally different guy had appeared for just a heartbeat, then completely vanished.

When class had finished, Mr Malik asked us to hang back for our extra work.

'Complete this assignment and bring me your answers in the morning,' he said, laying a sheet of paper on the desk.

When I picked it up, I found there was only one question written on the page: *Why do I enjoy science?*

'Is that it?' I asked. 'This'll take, like, two seconds.'

'And that is all the punishment you deserve,' he replied with a smile.

'Oh right . . . thanks,' I said, a bit confused. 'But . . . why are you letting us off so easy?'

'Because you do not deserve to be punished,' replied Mr Malik. 'If you did, I would punish you. But the headmaster is wrong.'

'Won't you get into trouble if he finds out?' I asked.

'I am giving you extra homework, just as I promised,' he replied. 'Though I never said it would be difficult. Sometimes, when dealing with a bully, the only option is to outsmart them.' And, with that, he turned away and began clearing the desks.

All the other kids had gone now, and they'd left their experiments all over the place. Mr Malik pottered from desk to desk, collecting the equipment into a box. I didn't know what the Agency were on about, but this guy didn't seem bad at all. They had to have their facts wrong. Maybe it was all just a mix-up and the real target was meant to be the headmaster . . . Something didn't feel right.

'I'm totally confused,' I whispered to Umer as we stood up to leave.

'I know,' he replied. 'He just seems . . . nice.'

We stopped at the door and looked back at Mr Malik. He was standing at the far end of the room now, fishing a set of keys out of his pocket with one hand, and clutching a box of lab equipment in the other. He unlocked the storeroom cupboard, stepped inside and went to pull the door closed behind him. But, in the last moment before his face vanished from sight, he looked straight at us, winked, and then was gone.

'Maybe they're right about him, and maybe they ain't,' I said, turning to Umer. 'But if we're gonna crack this thing, we're gonna have to start watching him round the clock. One lesson a day ain't gonna cut it.'

'But how?' replied Umer. 'He's gonna notice us if we just hang around outside his classroom. Plus, it seems like we don't exactly get a lot of time off here.'

'We'll just have to be sneaky about it. Create opportunities to get out of lessons. Take turns going for toilet breaks, fake being ill, that kind of thing.'

Umer opened his mouth to reply but all I heard was: '*Meeeooowwwwwwww* . . .'

'Uh . . . Umer, did you just meow?' I asked him.

'Of course not,' he said, looking as confused as me. 'It came from over there.' He pointed to the far side of the corridor, where a little air vent was cut into the wall at around knee height.

'*Meeeooowwwwwwww*,' squeaked the air vent.

'*Shhh*,' came a sharp reply from somewhere inside. *What the hell was going on?*

We wandered over and bent down to look through the grate. It was pitch black inside.

'Is someone there?' I asked.

There was a moment's silence, then . . .

'No,' came a little voice.

'Azrah?' I replied. 'Is that you?'

A face appeared in the vent.

'Hello,' said Azrah, grinning.

'What are you doing in the wall?' asked Umer.

'Visiting King Kong,' she replied, and brought her hands up towards the vent. Cradled in her fingers was a tiny kitten.

'*Meeeooowww,*' said King Kong.

'Whoa!' I gasped. 'Where'd you get him from?'

'Not "him". King Kong is a girl,' replied Azrah matter-of-factly. 'Her mama is in here too. Plus two brothers and one sister. I have been bringing them food. You won't tell, will you?'

'No way,' I answered. 'Why would we do that?'

'The headmaster cannot find out,' she said. 'He would do something terrible, I am sure.'

'Don't worry,' replied Umer. 'Your secret's safe with us.'

'Thank you,' she said, smiling. 'And . . . if you like . . . I can help you with your problem too.'

'Uh, what problem?' I replied nervously. *What had she heard?*

'I know the secret to this place,' replied Azrah. 'If you like, I will teach you.'

'Teach us what exactly?' I asked.

'How to become . . . *invisible.*'

CHAPTER TEN
UMER'S LOG

So, it turned out, Azrah didn't mean *literally* invisible. But she *did* have a way to get around the school unseen. And that was exactly what we needed.

'I saw her wandering around the yard on my first day,' explained Azrah as she carefully lifted off the loose air-vent cover round the back of the school building. 'King Kong's mama. She was very thin with a big fat belly. She was looking for somewhere safe to have her litter.'

'And you followed her in here?' I asked.

'Exactly. I have been coming back ever since.'

We followed Azrah into the vent. Once inside, she pulled the metal grate back into place behind us. She led us down a series of dark passages, hidden away behind the walls of the school. The only light shone through the air vents at our feet.

Before too long, Azrah came to a stop. 'Here,' she whispered, crouching down. There, in front of her, suckling away in the shadows, were four tiny kittens. They were curled up against their mother's belly, pummelling away with their little paws. The mother cat immediately began rubbing her head against Azrah's fingers and purring.

'This is Fizzy, this is Bano, this is Laddu, and you already know King Kong,' whispered Azrah, pointing at each of the little kittens in turn as she spoke. 'Their mama is called Chooha.'

Now I ain't one to get sentimental over cats, but these guys were pretty cute.

'Can we take one home?' whispered Umer, whose eyes were so wide he looked like a manga character.

'What are you talking about, man?' I hissed. 'You're meant to be on a mission. Would Jason Bourne take home a kitten?'

'He might . . .' replied Umer, stroking Laddu's little head with the tip of his finger. 'I think he'd choose this one.'

'Azrah,' I said, ignoring my idiot sidekick. 'You're a lifesaver. This is just what we needed.'

And it was. The air vents in the main building were easily big enough for us to stand up in and move around. Once you were in there, you could get almost anywhere in the school without being seen. Now the mission could really begin.

'So, why are you needing to watch Mr Malik?' asked Azrah, tickling Chooha's sand-coloured cheek.

'We can't really get into it,' I explained. 'But we just need to make sure he's a good guy.'

'He seems to be very nice,' replied Azrah.

'Yeah, I know what you mean,' I agreed. 'But we're kind of on a secret mission, so can you keep it to yourself?'

'Of course,' she said with a grin. 'What is said in the air vents stays in the air vents.'

Over the next week, we began spying on Mr Malik at every opportunity. And we got good at it too. Probably better than James Bond, I reckon. Sure, we didn't kill any bad guys or jump out of any planes, but we became experts at the sneaking bit. I got so good at sneaking out of class I could have taught a lesson in it – and then snuck out halfway through! We'd hide in the walls and watch Malik as he came and went from his classroom. Anywhere there was a vent, we could spy on him. And, as we did, day after day, we worked out exactly what kind of guy our target was: boring.

Man this dude was dull. He had no social life. He didn't hang out with any of the other teachers. He ate the same thing alone every day. He rarely left his classroom, apart from when he needed to sleep, or eat, or go to the loo. Umer got obsessed with that last bit and insisted on keeping track of how often Malik visited the toilet. (Every 1.5 hours for an average of 2.3 minutes, if you wanted to know. I didn't.) We discovered he was left-handed, he always carried a hanky, and he wore odd socks every single day – fascinating stuff, huh? In fact, the most exciting detail we learned about him was that he kept a packet of sweets, called Super Sours, in his desk drawer. (I may have helped myself to one – but just in the name of research . . .)

The only thing that was evil about this guy was how dull his life was. Seriously, the closest thing he had to a hobby was tidying up that storeroom of his. He was *ALWAYS* in there, cleaning and straightening the place. He must have kept it super neat, because it wasn't exactly huge. We'd only managed to sneak the odd glimpse inside before he pulled the door closed, and it looked smaller than my room back home (and that ain't much bigger than a fat guy's coffin). But it still took up almost all of his spare time. He was devoted to it. Hell, the guy treated that place better than my parents treated each other. If it was legal for a man to marry his cupboard, I wouldn't stand in the way.

'I don't think he's evil,' said Umer one lunchtime as we sat in the food hall eating. The 'food' was a kind of orange mush that tasted like burning tyres and I was struggling to make a dent in it.

'I know, right?' I replied. 'He's just some guy. Some boring, forgettable science guy.'

'Maybe we should tell the Agency he's not doing anything wrong?' suggested Umer. 'Maybe they'll let us go home if we do?'

'Yeah, that's true,' I agreed. 'They might convince our parents to let us out early.'

Umer nodded as he chewed his mush. He was quiet for a time.

'What is it?' I asked, cos I could see his little hamster brain was working away in there.

'Well . . .' he replied. 'There's just one thing that's bothering me.'

'The food, right? It tastes like an exhaust pipe.'

'No, not the food,' he said, bringing out his notebook. 'Take a look at this.'

'Ah, man, not your wees-and-poos diary,' I muttered, pushing my plate away. 'Why you so obsessed with Malik going to the toilet?'

'Toilet habits can teach you a lot about a person. I always know when my dad's stressed at work by how often –'

'OK, that's enough!' I interrupted. 'I don't need to know about your dad's irritable bowel.'

'Fine, but there's something going on here,' said Umer, pointing to a hand-drawn chart in the notebook. 'Mr Malik's pretty regular about going to the loo all through the day, see?'

'Uh-huh,' I replied, though I was shaking my head cos I couldn't believe we were looking at this again.

'And he always uses the staff toilet at the end of the hall, yeah?'

'Yeah, usually.'

'Right,' said Umer. 'Except for when he's cleaning the storeroom. When he's in there, he can go hours without using the loo.'

'So what? Maybe he's just dehydrated?'

'But he isn't, see?' said Umer, turning the page to reveal another chart, labelled MR M. BEVERAGE CONSUMPTION.

'You've been counting his drinks too?' I asked, surprised at how weirdly focused Umer could get if you stopped paying attention to him for a bit.

'Uh-huh,' he said with a smile.

It's funny, I somehow always manage to forget that Umer isn't actually as stupid as he looks. He just sees the world differently. Absorbs things differently. One minute he'll spot something I've totally missed, and the next he'll walk head first into a parking meter.

'That's how I know he definitely isn't dehydrated,' continued Umer. 'He had two cups of tea and half a litre of water just one hour before cleaning his storeroom cupboard for one hundred and twenty-seven minutes.'

'Fine, so he's getting his fluids. Good on him. I still don't see how this helps us.'

'Just look. Before entering the cupboard, he hadn't been to the toilet for one hundred and eighteen minutes. And, after exiting the cupboard, he didn't go again for another forty-one minutes. A total of two hundred and eighty-six minutes without a toilet break. Nearly five hours.'

'Why are you telling me this, man?'

'Because it can mean only one thing!'

'And what's that?'

'He's *peeing* in the cupboard!' replied Umer.

Huh . . . Was this really what it had come to? A week of our hardest efforts, and all we could tell the Agency was that our target was peeing in his cupboard?

'He's peeing . . . in . . . the cupboard?' I repeated slowly.

'Absolutely,' replied Umer with a serious expression. 'You can't change your toilet habits that much while still drinking all that liquid. And that means he has to be going to the toilet while he's in there with the door shut.'

'OK . . . fine . . . While that's definitely disgusting, I don't think the Agency are gonna consider it a crime against humanity.'

'Look, I know it's not much, but it's the only thing I can find that doesn't feel right. Maybe he's doing other things while he's in there.'

'Like a number two?'

'No! Experiments! Maybe that's where he works on his secret projects! It's not like we've ever actually been inside.'

That was true. We'd watched Malik go in and out dozens of times, but we'd never been able to get a proper look. He kept the door closed when he was in there and locked when he wasn't.

'OK,' I replied. 'How are we gonna get inside then?'

'Could we pick the lock?' suggested Umer.

'Pick the lock? Are you kidding? You can't even pick your nose without getting a nosebleed.'

'Yes I can!' he snapped. 'And we should at least give it a try.'

'What, picking your nose? No thanks, you can do that in your own time.'

'No! Picking the lock!' he said, starting to sound annoyed with me. 'They always do it in the movies with just a paper clip. It can't be that hard.'

'OK,' I replied. 'There's no harm trying. But just leave the lock-picking to me. You'd probably just give it a nosebleed.'

'FOR THE LAST TIME, I CAN PICK MY NOSE!' shouted Umer, and shoved a finger up his nostril to prove it.

★

Ten minutes later, after we'd cleaned up Umer's nosebleed, we snuck into the science room. Just as we'd expected, the place was deserted. The other students were off doing their lunchtime chores, and we'd just watched Mr Malik take a seat in the food hall with a plate of the same garbage that we'd been eating. There wasn't a man alive who could force down a portion of that weird orange gruel in less than fifteen minutes. That would buy us the time we needed.

'I think I saw some paper clips in his desk,' I whispered as we closed the door behind us. 'I'll grab a couple.' I ran over and pulled open the middle drawer. There, beside a packet of Super Sours, was a little red-and-white cardboard box with an image of a paper clip on the front. There were three left inside. I took two.

'Untwist them so they're straight,' said Umer, who was waiting by the storeroom door.

'I know, I know,' I said, hurrying over. 'I watch just as much telly as you do.'

I was about to insert the knobbly bits of wire into the lock when Umer stopped me. 'Wait!' he whispered, grabbing my arm.

'What?' I asked, looking about in panic.

Umer reached past me and tried the door handle. It was firmly locked.

'Nope,' he said with a shrug. 'Oh well.'

'Umer!' I hissed. 'Don't scare me like that. I thought we'd been rumbled.'

'Sorry,' he replied with a little grin. 'Worth a try though.'

Shaking my head, I took a deep breath and slid the wires into the lock. This was my chance to prove myself as a secret agent.

'Come on, Humza,' I whispered under my breath. 'You can do this . . .'

Yeah. Right.

Why do they make it look so easy on TV? I swear, picking locks is impossible! Five minutes later, I was still rattling those stupid bent paper clips around in the keyhole.

'Try turning it topwise,' said Umer, doing his impression of the least helpful person in the universe.

'Shut up, man!' I snapped, wiping the sweat from my forehead. 'That ain't helping.'

'Let me try then,' he said, reaching for the wires. 'I bet I can do it.'

'Give it your best shot,' I said, shaking my head. 'I quit.'

I handed Umer the paper clips and slid over to make room for him. He was just slipping the wires into the lock when there came a booming voice from behind us.

'STOP RIGHT THERE!'

We spun round to see the headmaster standing in the doorway, a furious look on his face. His eyes looked like they might explode. He was gripping the door handle so tight I could hear it rattling. I'd never seen him so angry.

'My office! Now!'

CHAPTER ELEVEN
THE RULER

Mr Mahmood didn't say another word to us as we made our way down the corridor towards his office. Any students we saw in the hallway, pushing mops or polishing wood, stopped and watched us in silence. It was like they could sense how bad this was. How much trouble we were in.

I suddenly remembered that I had Grandpa's phone in my bag. I could feel it clonking against my back as we marched down the hall. If Bald-head Mahmood searched us, there was no way I'd be allowed to keep it. This was bad. This was very bad . . .

Mr Mahmood walked straight into his office and took a seat. As we followed him in, my eyes fell immediately upon the photo on the desk in front of him. It was a framed picture of himself; he was sitting in the very same seat, right there at his desk, and frowning up at the camera. He was looking at the photographer in exactly the same way he was looking at Umer and me right now.

It was seriously weird. It was like having two Mr Mahmoods staring at you as you entered the room. Who the hell keeps a photo of *himself* on his office desk? Especially a photo of himself sitting *in* his office, in *exactly* the same position, pulling *exactly* the same face?

'Close the door behind you,' he said softly.

Ah, man . . . Shutting ourselves in a room with this guy just seemed like the worst idea ever. But what else could we do? I pulled the door closed. Mr Mahmood leaned back in his seat, interlocking his fingers across his belly.

'So, you wish to steal from me?' he said in the same strange tone – far softer than I'd ever heard him speak before. By that point, I think I'd have actually preferred him to start shouting at us. Anything would be better than the weird menacing thing he was doing right now. It was properly creepy.

'We weren't stealing,' I replied. 'I swear.'

'Oh really? I find you breaking into locked storage area, in room with no teacher, during lunch period, and you tell me this is not to steal?'

'We were just looking for Mr Malik, I promise.'

'I am no fool, boy,' he said, leaning forward, the anger beginning to rise in his voice.

I looked down at my feet. There was no way I was getting out of this.

'You have nothing more to say?' he asked.

I glanced at Umer. He was as stuck as I was. I looked back at my feet.

'That ruler on my desk,' said the headmaster, 'pass it to me.'

'What?' was all I could manage – he couldn't be serious . . . *Could he?*

'The ruler,' he said again. 'Pick it up and place it in my hand.'

'Can't we just clean more toilets?' I asked, starting to sound a little panicked.

'Fetch it now or I promise you it will be much, much worse,' said Mr Mahmood.

He wouldn't really hit us, would he? Mr Malik said they didn't use sticks for discipline any more. Surely the headmaster, of all people, wouldn't break that rule? He couldn't. Either way, there was no chance I was gonna pick that ruler up for him. He could just reach for it himself if he wanted it so badly. I wasn't gonna budge. I couldn't, actually. I don't know if it was fear or anger or what, but I just couldn't move an inch. I knew that every second I stood there the punishment would be getting worse, but I was frozen to the spot. I could feel the headmaster's eyes burrowing into me.

And then, before I realized what was going on, Umer grabbed for the ruler.

'It was my fault,' he said, placing it in Mr Mahmood's hand. 'Humza tried to stop me.'

'Umer! What are you –' I began, but he flashed

me a look so serious that the words caught in my throat.

'I see,' said the headmaster, staring at Umer. 'In that case, hold out your hand.'

Umer opened his fist and held out his palm. The headmaster turned to me. He looked right into my eyes – held my stare. He knew! He knew this was worse. He knew Umer was taking the blame for us both, and that my letting him do it was a special type of punishment, just for me.

'It's not Umer's fault!' I cried, jumping forward. 'I did it!'

But Umer interrupted me: 'Humza, stop,' he said. 'It was me. My idea. I'll take the punishment. You'll know when it's your turn to *take* something.' And, for just an instant, his eyes flashed from mine to the desk. I was so shocked by everything going on that, at first, I didn't get it. Umer did it again, just once more. His eyes flicked away, then back to me. He wanted me to see something. Mr Mahmood hadn't noticed. He was still staring at me with that nasty glint in his eye.

I glanced down in the direction Umer had indicated and saw immediately what he meant. Mr Mahmood's keys were lying right there, just inches from me, on the desk. I barely had time to look back up at Umer before the ruler came crashing down upon his open palm. In that brief instant before the impact, Umer smiled at me. *WHACK!*

I had to move fast. By taking the punishment like that, Umer had allowed me just the window I needed. I reached out a hand and snatched the keys off the desk. The moment I'd seen them, I knew what Umer was telling me. These were the keys to every door in the school – including every cupboard. And now they were ours! I stuffed them into my pocket before the headmaster noticed.

'I hope this has taught you a lesson,' said Mr Mahmood, straightening up again. 'Both of you.'

When we were back in the hallway, Umer kept his head lowered. He was blinking quickly and trying not to meet my eye. Umer and I had cried in front of each other a million times, but I could see how much he didn't want to cry right now.

'Are you OK?' I asked.

He swallowed, still clutching one hand in the other, then nodded. 'Did you get them?' he asked.

I looked about the hall to make sure we were

alone, then brought the key ring out of my pocket and held it up. The huge grin that spread across Umer's face squeezed a tear out of one of his eyes. It ran down his cheek and dropped on to his shirt.

'That was amazing, man,' I said. 'Seriously amazing. How did you think of that so fast?'

'I just saw them lying there,' he replied with a little smile. 'Anyway, it was teamwork.'

'Yeah, but I only took the keys. You did the brave bit,' I said, and I couldn't tell if his face flushed because of what had just happened or because of what I was saying.

'Come on,' he said with an embarrassed little grin. 'Let's go open that cupboard.'

The science-room cupboard looked exactly how you'd expect a science-room cupboard to look – which was itself unexpected, because by that point I'd been expecting more. I had hoped we'd find a secret workshop and a ton of weird gadgets scattered about. Instead, there were just textbooks, stationery supplies and a load of basic lab equipment like you'd get in any school.

'This can't be it,' I said, still not fully believing that our whole investigation had come to nothing.

'I was . . . I was wrong,' mumbled Umer, looking about the tiny room. 'He's not up to anything in here.'

'Sorry, man,' I said, patting him on the shoulder and turning back towards the classroom. 'It was a good theory though.'

'He isn't evil at all,' said Umer, following me out of the cupboard. 'He's just a science teacher. A normal boring science teacher.'

'Yup, and he'll be finished with his lunch real soon, so let's get the hell out of here before we get in trouble.'

I locked the door behind us and we began to walk towards the exit. 'We'll just tell the Agency that they were barking up the wrong –'

I never managed to finish that sentence. The noise stopped me dead –

Clunk . . . Thud . . . Hiiiiissssssssss!

It was coming from behind us. From the storeroom . . . the empty storeroom we'd just walked out of!

'It sounds like someone's in there,' said Umer.

'Quick! Hide!' I whispered. We ran to the only spot in the room that offered any cover: Mr Malik's desk. We ducked behind it just as the storeroom door began to open. Out of it stepped Mr Malik! How the hell had he done that? The room had been empty – I'd never been so sure of anything in my life! That was some Grandpa-level magic!

Mr Malik closed the cupboard door behind him, then paused and looked around. I could barely see him through a gap in the front of the desk, and I prayed that he couldn't see us. My heart was going like crazy. If he decided to sit down in his chair, we were done for.

Thankfully, after locking the storeroom door, Mr Malik headed straight for the exit. We heard him disappear off down the corridor. I didn't dare move an inch until the clicking of his heels on the stone floor had faded entirely.

'Did that just happen?' said Umer eventually.

'Uh-huh,' I replied.

'But . . . it was empty!'

'There must be another way in. A secret door!'

'Whoa,' gasped Umer. 'But . . . where?'

'We have to look again.'

'What if he comes back?'

'According to the schedule, he ain't got a class for another hour,' I said, jumping up. 'Maybe he's gone to find some better food?'

'I don't know, Humza.'

'Come on! We have to! We'll be quick.' I ran back to the cupboard and unlocked the door as fast as I could. Inside, it was exactly as it had been. Nothing was out of place. There were no other doors. It was still just a boring old store cupboard.

'All right,' I said. 'Start searching.'

'Where?' replied Umer, looking about.

'I don't know. In movies, you always pull on a book or play some notes on a piano.'

'I don't see any pianos.'

'Forget pianos. Try these books with me,' I told him, and I began pulling at the textbooks stacked on the shelves. Umer joined me, starting at the opposite side of the room. By the time we met up in the middle, we'd tugged on every last book, but none of them had revealed a secret door.

'I guess it's not the books then,' said Umer.

'There must be something!' I cried. 'Some sort of lever or button.'

We searched and searched. We picked up, pulled out and turned over everything we could find, but it was no good. There was no secret passage. No trigger. No switch.

'We'd better go,' said Umer. 'We're running out of time.'

'But I'm *sure* this is it! It has to be,' I replied.

'I know, but we need to hurry now. He could be back any second and we can't risk getting caught in here. We'd be trapped –'

The moment he said the words, it clicked.

'Umer!' I gasped. 'That's it! That's exactly what we want!'

'Huh?' he replied. 'You want to get *trapped*?'

'I've said it before and I'll say it again: you're a genius!'

'Um . . . thanks?' he said with a little smile. 'Why?'

'Trapped! Locked in! That's the trick!'

'What are you talking about?'

'When we got here, the door was locked, right? But it turned out Mr Malik was already inside. Which means he must have locked the door behind him. And who locks themself inside a store cupboard? No one! That's the secret! We need to lock ourselves in, like he did!'

I put the key back in the lock and twisted it – this time from the inside. The effect was immediate. A great *CLUNK* sounded and the whole floor beneath us juddered. Then came a dull *THUD* as we seemed to separate from the walls, sinking downward with a long, drawn-out *HIIIISSSSSSS*. It was an elevator! But, unlike normal, here only the floor moved. The rest of the room stayed above us, held fast to the walls.

'You did it!' gasped Umer. 'You figured it out! You *are* a real spy!'

'Yeah, boi!' I said, laughing. 'The name's Badman . . . Agent Badman.'

Umer's laugh echoed off the metallic walls as we descended deeper and deeper into the darkness.

CHAPTER TWELVE
ABOUT TIME

Down and down we drifted, until the storeroom above grew small and faint. It was like looking up from the bottom of a well. The silver walls of the lift shaft were slick and dark. There was no way of climbing out of this place.

At last, with a deep, echoing *thunk*, we came to an abrupt stop. Wherever we were, it was pitch black. The fluorescent tube lights in the storeroom high above had no effect down here at all.

'What now?' asked Umer, his face invisible in the gloom.

'I guess we look for a light switch,' I replied. I stepped forward, reaching my hands out to feel around for the walls. But there were no walls. I turned and tried the other way, reaching out behind me. Again, nothing. We were surrounded by total blackness in every direction.

'I don't like this,' said Umer, and I could hear the fear in his voice.

'It'll be OK,' I replied. 'We've just got to keep going.'

I took a small, careful step forward. Then another. Inching along through the void, I felt the floor beneath my feet change. I had stepped from the lift on to a slightly different surface, one that was a fraction lower – or maybe just made from a different material? Either way, I was in a bigger space than the storeroom – much bigger, judging by the echo of my footsteps. But, still, there was nothing around me to see or feel. Only blackness.

'Give me your hand,' I said, reaching back towards Umer. I felt about blindly until my hand connected with his. He took a careful step towards me. Then another –

As soon as he stepped off the platform and on to the floor of this larger room, we heard a loud clunk and a sharp hiss from the lift. The lights snapped on at once, just in time for us to see the elevator floor disappearing back up into the ceiling.

'Whoa . . .' I gasped, looking around the place.

This was it! This was *exactly* what we'd been looking for. I don't know a lot about being a genius inventor in hiding, but, if I was one, this was how I'd do it.

It was slick. Super slick. An ultra-modern lab, filled with all kinds of devices and computers, robot arms and complicated machinery. I honestly had no idea what I was looking at, only that it was like nothing I'd ever seen before.

'Do you think this is his secret lab then?' asked Umer.

'Nah, let's go,' I replied.

He looked at me for a moment, then we both burst out laughing.

'What do we do now?' he asked.

'I dunno. I guess we take a look around, see if we can figure out what he's been up to down here?'

'I wonder what this does?' said Umer, walking towards what looked like a robotic sheep with no head. He was just about to prod it when the sheep took a step back, apparently startled by Umer's approach.

'Argh!' cried Umer, leaping away.

'What are you doing, man? Leave that robo-sheep alone!'

'I didn't realize it was alive,' said Umer.

'For all we know, everything in here's alive. Just don't touch any of it.'

And, with that, I turned round and tripped straight over the sheep's power cable . . .

CRASH!

The big metal shelving unit I'd collided with was jam-packed with crazy-looking gadgets. They flew this way and that as the whole thing toppled over backwards. I reached out and tried to grab hold of the shelf but missed it by a mile. Instead, I managed to wrap my fingers round just one of the tumbling devices.

I squeezed my eyes shut and waited for the devastating clatter of a dozen inventions exploding on the stainless-steel floor. But it never came.

Very slowly I unclenched my eyes and looked around. Nothing had hit the ground. Nothing had exploded. Instead, it was all just floating in thin air. Even the shelving unit was just hanging there at an angle, completely frozen.

'Whoa . . .' I said, under my breath. 'Umer, check it out.'

But Umer didn't reply. I figured he must have been even more shocked than I was, until I turned round and looked at him. He was frozen too! He seemed to have been in the middle of turning to face me when the universe had hit pause.

I walked right up to him. 'Umer?' I said.

No reaction. He was absolutely still. His expression looked startled. The noise of me tripping into the shelf must have made him jump. What the hell had happened? What had caused the world to freeze?

And then it struck me. I looked down at the device gripped tightly in my hand. I'd totally forgotten about the one object I'd managed to catch. In my hand was a watch. And not a modern

one, not one you'd wear on your wrist. This was an old-fashioned-looking thing. A pocket watch, like they used to have in Victorian times. But it looked bigger and chunkier than any I'd ever seen in films. It was almost the size of a doughnut, with a brass-coloured body and a thin dome of glass protecting the delicate machinery within. And there wasn't just a single watch face on the front – there were a bunch of them. They were all different sizes and styles, and they were clustered round a big central face. At the top of the watch, there were a couple of little buttons and, between them, a twisty

metal knob. It looked like my thumb must have clicked on one of the buttons when I'd grabbed it in the fall. Without releasing my grip on the button, I lifted the watch to my ear. There was no ticking. None of the hands moved. The watch was frozen.

This was it! This was the reason time had stopped! Incredible! Mr Malik had built a time-freezing device and put it inside a pocket watch. Imagine what you could do with something like this! Imagine what you could get away with!

Then a thought struck me. *What if I'm stuck this way?*

I carefully lifted my thumb off the button to see if it would pop back up, but it didn't budge. I was just about to try pressing the button opposite, to see if that would *un*freeze time, when I stopped myself. What was I thinking? If I restarted time now, everything would smash on the floor. This had given me a chance to put right my mistake.

I began by straightening the shelves. They slid easily through the air as I lifted them. They felt almost weightless. And, when I let them go for a moment, they just hovered there, waiting to be moved again.

Once the shelves were straight, I began to replace the items I'd knocked over. One or two of them had been only millimetres from smashing on the ground when time had frozen. I scooped them all up and popped them back on to the shelves, hoping I was getting them in the right order.

When everything appeared roughly how it was meant to, I turned back to the watch. Here goes . . .

Click . . .

The instant I pressed the button, Umer turned round to face me. It was almost unnoticeable. A totally smooth transition. He just came back to life.

'What was that?' he said, looking puzzled.

'What was what?' I asked.

'I thought I heard a crash,' he said, sounding confused. 'Did you bump into something?'

'Uh . . . no . . .' I replied, trying to hide the little grin that was tugging at the corners of my mouth.

'What's that in your hand?' he asked, looking at the watch.

'This? Oh . . . uh . . . this makes your trousers fall down,' I told him.

'What?' he replied.

'Yeah, you just press this button, like so . . .'

As I said it, I clicked the little button. Instantly,

everything froze. But without the shelf falling and all those gadgets flying through the air, it was pretty hard to even tell. Umer just seemed like he was waiting for me to speak. But, if you looked real close, you could see it – he was absolutely motionless. He wasn't breathing or blinking or anything. A single bead of sweat was frozen in place, halfway down his cheek.

'Umer?' I said.

Nothing. He was a statue. I laughed and immediately pulled down his trousers, then hit the UNFREEZE button again.

'What do you mean it makes your . . .' he began, before looking down and noticing that his trousers were now round his ankles. 'Argh!' yelled Umer, stumbling backwards in shock towards another shelf full of inventions. I only barely managed to hit the FREEZE button before he smashed into the lot.

I grabbed Umer and pulled him away from the shelves, before resting him on the ground where he couldn't hurt himself or anything else. Then I restarted time.

'Argh,' screamed Umer, flailing his arms and legs around on the floor, like an upturned tortoise.

When he realized he wasn't actually falling, he

stopped and looked up at me. Then he looked down at his trousers, still round his ankles.

'What the hell just happened . . .' he mumbled.

I couldn't help but burst out laughing.

'Ah, man, I'm sorry,' I said, bending over double. 'I couldn't resist.'

'What was that?' said Umer as he slowly got to his feet.

'It's this!' I said, holding up the watch. 'This thing freezes time! The whole world freezes and then you can mess around with everything.'

'So you used it to pull down my trousers?' said Umer, sounding unimpressed as he tugged them back up.

'You gotta admit,' I replied, 'it was pretty funny.'

'Not as funny as when I do it to you!' he said, jumping up and grabbing for the watch.

'No way! It ain't yours!' I yelled, pulling it away from him.

But I wasn't quick enough and he already had his hand on it. We were both wrestling over the watch when it happened. I guess it was inevitable . . .

Click!

At first, you couldn't even tell anything had changed – we were still too busy fighting to notice that the world had frozen around us. But then Umer got a proper grip on the watch and prised it from my fingers. He lost his balance as he tore it away and stumbled backwards, right into that stupid robo-sheep.

The little headless creature was sent flying by the force of the collision. But instead of crashing into a wall or falling to the ground, it just hung there, floating in mid-air.

I looked at Umer. Umer looked at me. We both looked at the hovering sheep.

'Is this it?' he asked. 'Did we just freeze time?'

'Yeah,' I replied. 'But you ain't frozen. Why aren't you frozen?'

'Maybe that's how it works,' he said. 'If you're touching it when you click the button, you don't freeze?'

'This. Is. Awesome,' I replied.

'It's the best thing ever,' agreed Umer, staring at the watch in his hand. 'How do I unfreeze it? Is it this one?'

'Wait!' I yelled.

'What?' he replied, looking a bit surprised.

'First, put that sheep back where it came from. Otherwise it's gonna fly across the room when you restart time.'

Umer grabbed the sheep and popped it back in the same spot we'd first found it.

'OK, now click the other button,' I told him. 'The one on the right.'

Umer pressed the second button, and the watch's hands began to tick once again. Time had restarted.

'OK, now give it back before you get us into any more trouble,' I said, reaching out towards him.

'Just one thing first,' said Umer with a grin.

'No!' I shouted, but I was too slow.

Click . . .

Next thing I knew, I was standing there with my finger up my nose. Umer was cracking up.

'Hey!' I shouted, pulling my finger out of my nostril. 'That ain't cool!'

'If you didn't like *that*, then it's probably best if you don't look down,' said Umer, tears of laughter rolling down his face.

I looked down and realized my trousers were round my ankles.

'Umer!' I shouted, yanking them up.

'What?' he replied, grinning. 'It's only fair.'

'Fine, but that's enough. No more using it on each other.'

'Deal,' he replied and handed me the watch. 'So what do we do with it now?'

'Well,' I replied, 'when it comes to a device this powerful, you absolutely, positively have to do the right thing.'

'What? Hand it in to the Agency?' suggested Umer.

'No, man,' I replied with a grin. 'Mess with people!'

CHAPTER THIRTEEN
THE WATCH

So, yeah, I know, I'm a trainee secret agent on my first big mission – super important, super serious, my big break etc., etc. – BUT, let's not forget, I'm also me. I ain't too big to admit that I may have got a little bit caught up in the excitement of finding a time-freezing pocket watch and forgotten what I was meant to be doing. But are you telling me you wouldn't have done the same? Exactly!

After we'd found a button to call the lift back down, Umer and I headed up to the school. Thankfully, we didn't run into Malik along the way – but, even if we had, everything seemed different now. Less scary. With this incredible little hunk of metal in my pocket, we were unstoppable. Now we really could go anywhere unseen.

'Who shall we test it on?' asked Umer as we stepped out of the main building and into the yard.

I didn't even have time to reply before Sergeant Shah rolled into view. The psychotic PE teacher was sitting in his electric golf cart, shouting at a group of twenty or so exhausted-looking kids halfway through their 'midday-sun fun run'.

'Worthless!' bellowed Sergeant Shah through his megaphone. 'Useless! Pathetic!'

We watched him roll past.

'You know,' I said, turning to Umer, 'I never did like that guy.'

'Me neither,' agreed Umer, not taking his eyes off the doughy little man in the golf cart. 'Someone ought to teach him a lesson.'

He didn't need to say it twice. I held out the watch, Umer placed his hand on top, and . . .

Click . . .

Sergeant Shah's golf cart stopped in its tracks. All the jogging kids hung frozen in the air, beads of sweat hovering around them like tiny crystal balls, glinting in the sunshine.

'What shall we do to him?' asked Umer.

'I think I've got an idea,' I replied, nodding over to where a group of kids were on roof-repair duty.

One boy was halfway up a ladder, and a bunch of others were scattered here and there along the school's low roof. Each of them was carrying a bucket of hot melted tar and a sticky black paintbrush. Before we'd stopped time, they'd been using that tar to plug little holes all over the roof so the rain couldn't get in. That tar was the nastiest, stickiest stuff in the world. And it was just what we needed. When he saw what I meant, Umer grinned.

'Let's do it,' he said.

Five minutes later, once everything was set up exactly how we wanted it, we stepped back into the same spot we'd been in when time had frozen. Everything looked pretty much as it had done. In fact, if you'd been standing nearby, watching the whole thing play out in real time, you wouldn't even have noticed anything had changed. But it had . . .

'Ready?' I said to Umer.

'Ready,' he replied.

Click . . .

Everything burst back into life. The runners ran. The roof-repairers repaired. And Sergeant Shah shouted.

'You wretched worms! You call that running? I could run faster on my hands!' he yelled, shaking his fist so violently that his whole belly wobbled. 'If you don't speed up, I shall run down the lot of you!'

And, as he said it, he shoved one stubby little foot on to the accelerator pedal. There was a loud squelch and the cart took off like a rocket.

'*Aarghhh!*' screamed Sergeant Shah. 'My foot! My foot is stuck!'

The little vehicle was accelerating so quickly it threw him back in his seat. Kids dived in every direction as the PE teacher screamed towards them. And, no matter how hard he tried, he just couldn't take his foot off the accelerator pedal. It was as though someone had covered it in hot, sticky roofing tar.

Now, I don't know if you've ever seen a golf cart going at full speed, but those things can move. They look slow when rich old white guys are driving them around their country clubs in American movies – but I've seen some stunt guys doing tricks with them on YouTube, and they can go pretty fast when you floor it. And that's exactly what Sergeant Shah had done.

'*Aarrgghhhhhh!*' shouted Sergeant Shah, whizzing past us, zigzagging this way and that.

The golf cart shot through the school yard, sending kids running for their lives and firing up a cloud of dust. Sergeant Shah managed to avoid crashing into the main building by turning the cart just in time. He rocketed off in the other direction, screaming all the way. But there's only so long you can drive at that speed if you ain't spent your childhood playing Mario Kart. And, unfortunately for him, Sergeant Shah had wasted his youth on physical exercise and discipline.

As the other kids watched in stunned surprise, the golf cart shot up the small hill separating the main yard from the fields. Sergeant Shah was going so fast that the little slope acted just like a ramp, firing him up into the air.

'Whoa!' gasped Umer as the golf cart's wheels left the ground. It must have cleared fifteen feet. For a brief, beautiful moment, Sergeant Shah was actually flying! But, unfortunately for the heavyset PE teacher, what goes up must come down. And, with a crash of wood and a screech of metal, the cart smashed straight into the goat pen, disappearing in a cloud of dust.

Sunny, the school goat, was standing to one side watching all of this unfold. He tilted his head slightly, a curious expression on his face. 'Meh,' said Sunny, and went back to chewing some hay.

A moment later, Sergeant Shah came staggering out of the shed, covered from head to toe in something so foul-smelling I ain't even gonna try to describe it here. Let's just say that the kids on goat-cleaning duty hadn't been round yet.

'Wow. That was even better than I hoped,' said Umer, with a grin.

'I know,' I replied, laughing. 'I think I'm actually starting to enjoy summer school.'

'Ha, me too!'

'OK, so who's next?' I asked.

The smile slipped a little from Umer's face.

'I think I know,' he replied.

We found the headmaster in his office, sitting at his desk beside that weird self-portrait of his. We'd already stopped time before we let ourselves in. It was weird seeing people frozen like that, almost like visiting a waxwork museum. You could get right up in their faces. I couldn't help giving him a prod on the nose. It was like squidging plasticine:

his nose stayed where I smooshed it, all squashed up to one side.

'So, what do you want to do?' I asked Umer, who was standing with his arms folded a few feet away, staring at the headmaster. Umer picked up the picture on the desk and examined it for a moment. Then he reached for a thick black marker pen, popped off the cap and began to draw.

'Is that all?' I asked. 'You just want to ruin his picture?'

'No,' he replied, nodding to the rest of the room. 'You can get started on that lot.'

I looked around and realized that there were pictures everywhere, all over the walls. Tons of them. And they were *all* of Mr Mahmood. Here he was next to a birthday cake with a load of candles in it. There he was with Sunny the school goat. And in that one he was beside a statue of some great big swords. One just showed him in front of the school. Another was of him on holiday, alone somewhere . . . and that's when it struck me. He was alone in all of them (unless you count Sunny the goat, but even Sunny didn't look massively pleased to be hanging out with the headmaster).

Serves you right, I thought as I grabbed another

pen off the desk and began scribbling on a picture of the headmaster at the zoo. If you act so mean, of course you're not gonna have any friends. This guy deserved to be lonely.

After he'd finished defacing the desk picture, Umer joined me in scribbling on the rest of them. Together, we worked our way through every picture in the room. We added funny haircuts, scars, eyepatches; we gave him missing teeth, big ears, massive eyebrows; we did every single thing you can do to a photo to make it ugly. By the time we were done, we were cracking up just looking at our artwork.

A moment before we left the room, when every picture had been scribbled on in some way or other, Umer stopped in his tracks and turned back.

'Hold up,' he said. He walked towards the headmaster's desk and paused right in front of him. He picked up the marker pen again and began to write something, right in the middle of the headmaster's big bald head. His *actual* head! I couldn't quite make out what he'd written from where I was standing. It didn't look like English though.

When Umer was done, he slipped the pen back in the pot, took the ruler from where it lay on the desk, snapped it in two over his knee, then placed the pieces back down.

'OK,' he said, walking past me. 'Let's go.'

We found a good hiding place behind a big bin outside Mr Mahmood's office.

'You ready?' I said, holding up the watch.

Umer nodded. I pressed the button.

For a moment, nothing happened. There was only the hum of insects outside and the soft ticking of the watch. Neither of us spoke. We just stared at the headmaster's door, waiting. We never even glanced at each other. We just held our breaths. I could feel my heart thumping in my chest. And then . . .

'*WHAAAAATTTT?!?!?!*' came the booming yell from the headmaster's room. '*WHAT? WHO? HOW?*' he bellowed. Then the door burst open. The headmaster looked like a charging bull. His eyes were pulsing with red veins. Every muscle in the top half of his weird muscly body was bunched so tight that he looked like he might snap, or just explode. His hands were shaking. His teeth were grinding into each other so hard I thought they'd pop. He looked around like a wild animal. A wild animal with the word 'KHOTA' written on its head in thick black marker pen.

'Ha! Donkey!' I said, laughing as quietly as I could.

Before Mr Mahmood could spot us, we ducked behind the bin, creasing up. Though Umer wasn't making a sound, I could feel his shoulders shaking with laughter. It was weird, but for the first time since we'd got here I wasn't scared of Mr Mahmood. I mean, what could he do to us now? With the watch, we were untouchable.

'*Raarrrgghhh!*' yelled the headmaster, before storming off down the corridor, looking for whoever could be responsible.

'Serves you right, Baldy,' I said, and we both burst out laughing.

Once the coast was clear, we came out from behind our bin. 'Well,' I said, still grinning, 'I guess we'd better tell the Agency what we've discovered.'

'Yeah,' replied Umer. 'They're going to want to hear about that lab.'

I was just about to put the watch in my backpack for safekeeping when I heard a sound that sent a chill through me.

'Hello, boys,' came the familiar voice.

We spun round. It was the last person in the world we wanted to run into.

'Well, well, well,' said Mr Malik. 'I see you've been trespassing.'

CHAPTER FOURTEEN
MEETING MR MALIK

Once, when I was small, I went down to the park with my dad, just before dawn. He was fasting for Ramadan, so had woken up super early to eat. The sun wasn't even up yet and it felt like there was no one else in the world but us. Everything was so silent. The thing I remember most though was the surface of the pond. It was absolutely still. A huge dark mirror. My dad said it was because the wind comes with the sun. With the heat of the day. I couldn't take my eyes off that flat black surface. I felt frozen just looking at it.

I saw the same stillness in Mr Malik's eyes that afternoon as he stared down at us in the silent hallway. Something beyond calm. Something bottomless and black. Everything about him had changed. All the kindness in his smile had been replaced by something hard. The warmth in his tone had vanished. His disguise had been dropped. It was like meeting someone's evil twin.

'You shouldn't have gone down there,' he said, taking a step towards us.

I glanced over at Umer. He looked frightened. It dawned on me that we had no idea who this guy really was. Yeah, he seemed nice during lessons, but maybe that was all part of his disguise? He didn't look at all like our friendly science teacher any more. He looked dangerous.

'You shouldn't have been prying,' he continued.

'What are you talking abou–' I began, but he cut me off.

'Did you really think I wouldn't be aware of intruders? Had you not even considered that I might have set an alarm or two?'

'We were just playing,' I said, taking a step back. 'It was an accident.'

'No,' said Mr Malik, 'it wasn't. That isn't a place one can find by accident. Which means you must have been looking for it. You knew it was there.'

Damn, this guy was smart. I needed to convince him that he was wrong. I had to.

'Mr Malik,' I said, looking him straight in the eye. 'I swear, we were just playing hide-and-seek. We found a key to the cupboard and it seemed like a great hiding place. But then the floor started moving and we ended up in your basement. That's all, I promise.'

There was a moment's silence as he stared at me. Absolute focus. Those intense eyes. Tiny movements in each pupil, like he was reading my every thought.

'If you were searching for it,' he continued, ignoring my attempt at a cover-up, 'then someone must have sent you. The question is, who?'

'Honestly, I have no idea what you're –'

'The Agency,' he hissed, cutting me off again. 'Of course. I was a fool to think they might leave me in peace. They really can't bear to lose even a morsel of control, can they?'

I couldn't speak. How was he doing this? No one's that smart. He was just working everything out by looking at us. I wanted to hide my face so he couldn't keep doing it.

'What's the Agency?' asked Umer, who was a natural when it came to playing dumb.

'Oh, be quiet,' snapped Mr Malik. 'The game's

up, boys. You're caught. I presume it was Agent Akbar who recruited you? Or was it that old fool Khan? Surely he must be dead by now. If not, he soon will be.'

I gasped. He was talking about Grandpa!

'Oh, so you *do* know who I'm talking about then?' said Mr Malik with a grin. 'Old Agent Grandpa's still kicking around, is he? Perhaps I should pay him a visit. Get the answers out of him that you two won't give me.'

'No!' I yelled. 'Leave Grandpa alone.'

'So you'll talk then, will you?' said Mr Malik. 'Good. Why did they send you here?'

'They –' I began, but I stumbled over the words. 'They just . . . needed to know you weren't working on anything dangerous. They'll back off if you talk to them.'

'Talk to them? Why would I talk to them? It makes far more sense just to eradicate them entirely.'

'What?' I gasped. 'You can't hurt the Agency. They're much too powerful.'

'Oh, I can assure you – that hasn't always been the case. In fact, I'm struggling to recall why I didn't squash them when I had the chance. Still, it looks like you two are just the motivation I needed to tie up loose ends. It's about time I wiped out your little Agency once and for all.'

'You can't!' I yelled. 'You won't be able to!'

'I most certainly can. Once I've dealt with the pair of you, I shall simply obliterate the Agency from history. It will be as though they never existed. Won't that be nice?'

'We won't let you,' shouted Umer.

'Oh? And how exactly do you intend to stop me?' Malik asked with a cruel grin.

'With this!' I yelled, whipping out the pocket watch from behind my back.

Mr Malik's face froze. It was as though I'd already pressed the button – but I hadn't touched it. Ha! We had him and he knew it!

'You foolish child,' he said in a tone that sent a chill through me. 'You have no idea what you're holding.'

'I know that, one click, and you'll freeze stiffer than a dead penguin,' I replied, my thumb hovering over the button.

'Is that what you think you've found? Some toy that freezes time? Fools! It *is* time. Now give it to me before you kill us all.'

I don't know how I knew, but I could tell that

he wasn't lying. I had a sickening feeling that I'd underestimated the heavy chunk of metal in my hand. Suddenly, I just wanted to get rid of the thing. But that wasn't an option. The Agency had been right all along – Malik was dangerous. I couldn't let him anywhere near the watch.

'Give it to me now, Humza,' he said, taking a step towards me. There was something in his eye that I'd not seen before. It looked like . . . fear? He was afraid of the watch – of what it could do.

I took a step back. 'Don't come any closer!' I shouted. I felt my backpack press up against the wall. I couldn't go any further.

'The watch,' said Mr Malik. 'Give me the watch.'

'No way!'

'Humza!' cried Umer. 'Do something!'

'*Give it to me!*' yelled Malik.

'*No!*' I shouted, and I brought my thumb down towards the button –

It all happened so fast. There was a flash at Malik's wrist and instantly my body felt like pure electricity. Every muscle in me tightened. My legs, my arms, my fingers – everything clenched in shock. Whatever futuristic weapon it was that he'd zapped me with, it had done the job. I'd failed to stop time. And, worse than that, I'd let go of the watch.

I didn't even realize until I saw it flying through the air. Mr Malik leapt forward, desperate to grab it, but he wasn't close enough. It was starting to tumble towards the stone floor.

I was still reeling from the shock. My muscles were on fire, my limbs rigid, I couldn't move an inch. But Umer saw what was happening and he dived. Somehow, we both knew we couldn't let that thing hit the ground. It was our only way to stop Malik. If it broke, we were done for.

It took everything I had just to drop to my knees and force my hand out in front of me. Umer was at my side, his fingers almost beneath the watch. My knuckles scraped over the stone tiles as I stretched for it. It was almost in my grip. *Almost* . . .

CRUNCH!!!

The pocket watch slammed into the floor. Our hands wrapped round it just a heartbeat too late. The glass shattered. The metal casing caved inwards. And, from somewhere deep inside the delicate machinery, a blue–white light exploded out in every direction.

It was like a million camera flashes had fired at

once. I shut my eyes as tight as I could, but the light was still blinding. There was a rush of noise that made my head feel like it might burst. It was too bright, too much to process. Screeching, burning, falling, turning – I felt like I'd fallen out of the universe.

And then, as quickly as it had begun, it was over. Umer and I were lying in the dirt, still clinging to the watch. The battered, cracked device was fizzing and hissing with blue–white sparks. Little slivers of lightning danced around our fingers, crackling softly. But they didn't burn. They felt almost cold. The hands on the watch's half-dozen faces were all spinning and twisting, racing backwards and forwards, stopping and starting. The thing was a mess.

'What the hell just happened?' I groaned. My head was spinning. Everything hurt. Looking down at the watch in our hands, I could barely tell which fingers were mine and which were Umer's.

'Where are we?' he replied, sounding as battered as I felt.

I craned my neck up to see.

Huh?

I scrunched my eyes up tight – then opened them again. It wasn't possible . . . It just couldn't be . . .

'Where's the school?' I mumbled.

It was gone. Totally gone. No buildings, no people, no Malik. We were outside in the forest. Nothing around us but trees and rocks and sky.

Umer let out a loud groan. 'I don't know what

you're groaning about,' I said. 'I'm the one Malik zapped.'

'I didn't groan,' replied Umer. 'I thought you did.'

We stared at each other. Neither of us made a sound. Someone behind us was breathing very loudly. Slowly, we looked round . . .

You'd have thought that with all the surprises of the last year (alien invasions, killer aunties, secret agents, time-freezing watches . . .) there wouldn't be much left that could shock me. But, I tell you, nothing, and I mean *nothing in the world*, could have prepared me for the heavy-breather standing behind us . . .

Seven feet tall, twice as long and uglier than my uncle Rabi after his hair plugs – whatever this thing was, it was staring straight at us. Its bright yellow eyeballs were the size of my fist, and there were stubby little horns sticking out from its skull like a crown. It lowered its massive domed head to get a better look at me. I couldn't breathe.

'D-d-d–' stammered Umer.

I think the word he was looking for was *dinosaur* . . .

CHAPTER FIFTEEN
TIME TROUBLE

'H-h-hi there,' I stammered to the creature standing over us. It was the best I could come up with in the circumstances and I immediately regretted it. Not just cos it was a pretty stupid thing to say to a dinosaur, but because straight away it was clear that old Dome-Head didn't much like the sound of my voice. In an instant, its curious-cow expression vanished. It raised its head, breathed in, and then *screamed* right in our faces.

I'd have said 'roared', but it wasn't exactly a roar. It was somehow high and deep all at once – the kind of sound you'd expect to hear if you were doing dentistry on a moose. I didn't know if he was going to eat us or just stomp us to death but, all of a sudden, lying on the ground didn't seem like a good idea.

My legs might not have been working properly a few seconds ago, but nothing gets you back on your feet like a dinosaur screaming in your face. Umer and I were up and running for dear life in a heartbeat. And, because neither of us had let go of the watch yet, it meant we were basically holding hands. Now it's worth pointing out that Umer ain't one of life's natural sprinters, and I was pretty much having to drag him along behind me. But, even so, I reckon I could have given Usain Bolt a run for his money that day (as long as he had also had to lug around a plus-sized Pakistani kid).

And it turns out, as luck would have it, our not letting go of the watch would be the best decision we'd ever made. Because just as that big ugly creature was gaining on us, the watch began to spark and fizz again. Dazzling blue light started dancing round our fingertips, brighter and brighter, tingling cold. Then, just like before, a blinding flash exploded out from the device. Light engulfed us all over again and, for an instant, the universe vanished . . . Only this time, it cleared even quicker, as though we'd sprinted right through the light and out the other side.

Now everything had changed again: we weren't in the forest any more – there was no forest. There was only charred concrete and metal scattered everywhere. The sky was blood red. There was a burnt, almost chemical, taste in the hot, dry wind. I spun round to look behind me. Old Dome-Head had disappeared.

'What the hell's going on?' I gasped.

'I dunno,' said Umer, 'but, whatever it is, it's just happened again.'

We didn't have time to wonder for long though. Turns out we still weren't alone. Thirty metres away, a bunch of soldiers were running towards us, shouting and firing laser weapons. I spun round to see what they could be shooting at. Coming from the other direction were a squad of scary-looking robot dudes, firing guns of their own. And Umer and I were caught right in the middle!

'*Aarghhh!*' cried Umer, diving on to the dirt and taking me with him. Laser bolts burst over our heads. 'Don't let go of the watch!' I shouted. 'Whatever you do, don't let go of the watch!'

The damaged device was starting to crackle again. We had to make sure we hung on to it. We couldn't risk getting separated. I never thought I'd say this, but Umer and I had to keep holding hands!

Just as we were about to get stomped on by futuristic army guys and killer robots, the blue–white light flashed again and, instantly, everything changed . . .

The concrete and metal were gone; the soldiers had vanished. The sky was now a deep clear blue and everything was silent.

'Thank God,' I said, pulling myself up.

'Yeah,' replied Umer. 'I thought we were goners for a minute there.'

'Lucky break, huh?' I said with a smile as we turned round –

BOOM!

Now I've seen plenty of volcanoes on TV and in movies, but it just ain't the same as having one erupt in your face. I mean, seriously. Damn . . . this big Mount-Doom-looking thing must have been over a mile away, but it still blew us off our feet. We crashed on to our backs in the dirt, the air knocked from our lungs.

'*Owww* . . .' groaned Umer. 'My pancreas.'

'What the hell's a pancreas?' I wheezed.

'Dunno,' he replied. 'But everything else hurts, so that probably does too.'

I would have laughed if it weren't for two things. First, my whole body felt like I'd gone over Niagara Falls in a tumble dryer. And, second, I'd just spotted the massive hunk of flaming rock that was hurtling through the sky towards us . . .

'Uh-oh . . .' I croaked.

'Oh no . . .' moaned Umer.

There was nowhere to run. No time to get out of the way. It was coming right for us. And this thing was huge – easily as big as the Chicken Cottage by the old swimming pool (and just as likely to kill you).

I shut my eyes as tight as I could and waited for the impact – but it never came. The rock never landed. Instead, just at the last moment, there was another bright flash. Even through my scrunched-up eyelids it was blinding.

When I dared to look, the volcano was gone.

We'd jumped again! But we weren't out of trouble yet . . . Cavemen. Definitely cavemen. They were staring straight at us. Running straight for us. Holding up spears. And clubs. And axes! I screamed. Umer screamed . . .

And then it happened again. A big white flash and suddenly we were on a building site. Some guys in hard hats were squatting nearby, drinking chai and staring over at us.

Then, *flash*, we were gone again. Now we were standing beside some cows. Next we were in the middle of a forest fire. After that we were deep under water. An instant later and we were back on dry land, surrounded by wild dogs. The next we were gone again. We just kept jumping and jumping – faster and faster with every flash.

'HUMZA!' shouted Umer between jumps. It was happening so fast now he only managed to shout one word each time we leapt. 'MAKE!' he yelled –

Flash!

'IT!' he shouted –

Another *flash* –

'STOP!' he cried – before another flash, and another, and another.

The effect was like a strobe light. I had no idea where we were or what was going on. There were glimpses of passing scenes: day, night, hot, cold, terrible storms, beautiful skies . . . I didn't know what I could do to make it stop, but I couldn't let go of the watch and risk Umer jumping without me. So I did what my dad had taught me to do whenever the TV signal was playing up during the cricket: I smashed my fist down on the watch as hard as I could.

BANG!

Everything stopped. Silence. We were back on a hill in the forest. There was no one and nothing around us. Just trees and rocks and the hum of nature. We looked down at the watch clasped tight in both our hands. The fizzing electricity had disappeared. The watch's hands were no longer moving. It was dead.

'Did we just . . .' began Umer, nervously.

'Time-travel?' I replied. 'Yeah, I think so.'

'Where are we?' he asked.

'Or when?'

'I can't believe he actually built a time machine.'

'Yeah, and we broke it,' I replied. 'We could be anywhere. Any . . . time.'

'I just hope we're not back in Dinosaur World,' said Umer, sounding worried. 'I didn't like Dinosaur World.'

I was about to agree when I saw it. Through a gap in the trees overhead, a long thin vapour trail was slicing its way through the bright blue sky.

'A jet!' I yelled, pointing to the distant plane. 'A jumbo jet! We're home!'

'What? Are you sure?' said Umer, still sounding too anxious to share my excitement.

'Yeah, look,' I replied. 'Down there!'

Far below us in the valley, we could just make out a dusty little house. And, not too far from that, there was another. And, next to that one, more and more houses. And there was a market square and a little mosque with its crescent-moon minaret. And people! Tiny colourful specks going about their days.

'The village!' I shouted. 'My dad's village! We're back!'

'Oh, thank God,' said Umer, smiling. He heaved

a big sigh of relief and, for the first time since he'd caught it, he released his grip on the broken watch.

I slid my backpack off and slipped the shattered watch inside it. I took a look at Grandpa's phone. No signal. It was useless up here in the hills. I shoved it back into my bag, beside the charger and the smashed-up watch.

'We need to move,' I said. 'We have to let the Agency know that Malik's planning to wipe 'em out. There's bound to be a phone down there we can use.'

'It looks a long way,' replied Umer.

'Then we'd better get going,' I told him.

CHAPTER SIXTEEN
THE CAVE

Bit of advice for you before you think about taking a ten-mile stroll through the forests of Pakistan in the heat of the midday sun. Don't. Stay home. Watch *Bake Off*. Seriously. It ain't worth it.

Now I'm not going to spend too much time telling you just how much this sucked. Doing so would only shorten both of our lives. Instead, I'll just give you the highlights.

Thirty minutes in . . .

    Umer spots a snake on the path and yells 'SNAKE!', causing me to jump off a small cliff and into a thorn bush. (Snake turns out to be a twig.)

Ninety minutes in . . .

Chased by a wild boar and end up
hiding in a tree until boar gets
bored and takes a nap.

Three hours in . . .

Umer begins hallucinating a giant
talking Pepsi bottle named Patrice.
They end up having an argument
and fall out with each other. Umer's
quiet after that.

Four hours in . . .

We encounter the waterfall . . .

'Whoa,' I gasped, staring over the edge of the cliff and down into the crashing white foam of the waterfall below.

'That's pretty high,' said Umer, leaning out beside me. 'How are we gonna get down?'

'Dunno, but we're so close,' I replied, pointing. 'Look.'

Just ahead of us, and far below, the river curled away through the trees and into the outskirts of the village. We'd made it so close only to be faced with a hundred-metre drop at the very end.

'Do you think the water's deep enough to jump?' said Umer.

'From a hundred metres up? No chance. Look at those rocks. You'd be shredded. I might survive, but you'd definitely be shredded.'

The waterfall was smashing down on a mass of jagged rocks far below us. There was no safe landing to be had there.

'We'll just have to go round then,' said Umer, looking out along the cliff.

'It could be miles,' I told him. 'We haven't got any food or water. And it'd definitely be dark before we made it to the village. You wanna spend the night out here?'

'No way,' said Umer, sounding nervous. 'But what else can we do?'

I didn't want to say it. I even whipped out Grandpa's phone again to check for a signal. Still nothing. I put the phone back in my bag and turned to Umer. We had no choice – there was only one way down.

'We climb,' I said.

'Climb?' he gasped. 'How can we climb? I've never even made it all the way across the monkey bars!'

'Yeah, but only cos you've never had the proper motivation.'

'But what if we fall? We could die!'

'That sounds like pretty good motivation to me,' I replied with a grin. 'Plus, it beats being eaten by wild animals in the dark, doesn't it?'

'I don't know, Humza.'

'Well, I tell you what,' I said, grabbing hold of a thick vine that was dangling over the edge. 'I'll start climbing down while you have a think about it all. I imagine the snakes will respect your personal space while you weigh up the options.'

Funnily enough, Umer didn't spend too much time thinking it through after that. Thirty seconds later, we were scaling the cliff face.

The drop couldn't have been more than a hundred metres, but it was straight down and the going was slow. The lower we got, the fewer vines there were to hang on to. We made sure to climb a few metres away from the flow of the waterfall, as the rocks there were drier and offered a better grip. But the further we went, the more water was being thrown up into the air. Before long, a fine mist was starting to cling to our skin. It felt amazing after five hours trekking in the heat – it was like nature's air con. But it also meant that the rocks we were holding on to were getting gradually more slippery with every step.

It was bound to happen sooner or later. And then it did. Umer's foot slipped from beneath him. He cried out as his fingers grabbed at thin air, but it was no use – he was falling.

'Umer!' I yelled as he plummeted downward, crashing into a rocky outcrop a few metres below. The impact knocked the wind from him, and he bounced into the waterfall, vanishing from sight.

'Umer!' I cried out again.

There was no reply – only the rush of water all around me. I couldn't see him anywhere. Not in the waterfall, not among the rocks below. He was gone. My heart was pounding. It was all my fault! I'd forced him to make the climb!

And then I heard it.

'Humza?' came a distant, echoey voice. 'You gotta check this out.'

As fast as I could, I clambered down to the rocky ledge that Umer had smashed into before vanishing. When I got there, I discovered that it stretched out in both directions along the cliff face, forming a rough path. Ahead of me, in the direction of the falls, the ledge seemed to disappear behind the powerful flow of water. As I followed it inwards, my back pressed to the rock, the path led me right into the roaring heart of the falls.

Within a few steps, the cliff face opened out into a large dark cave, totally invisible behind the waterfall. And, standing in the middle of it, looking slightly roughed up and a bit wet, was Umer. He had a big grin on his face.

'Umer!' I cried. 'You ain't dead! And you found a secret cave!'

'Yeah!' he said, laughing. 'Isn't it cool?'

'Yeah, it's awesome,' I replied.

'No, I mean, *cool*. Cold. It's like being in a fridge!'

He wasn't wrong. I could have stayed in there forever. 'Looks deep,' I said, staring into the darkness.

Further back, there were big boulders scattered around, and who knows what beyond them. Bears maybe? I wondered how many people had found this place over the years, and how many had been eaten. After we'd cooled off a bit, we made our way back out to the spot where Umer had first crashed, on the narrow ledge. As we followed the path in the opposite direction, away from the mouth of the cave, it seemed to form a crooked little track leading down into the valley. It was a bit rough in places, zigzagging along the face of the cliff, but it turned out to be just what we needed – a shortcut right to the ground!

Before long, we were standing beside the river, staring up at the waterfall, grinning like idiots. It was stunning from down here. And loud.

'I love it!' shouted Umer over the crashing of the water on the rocks.

'Me too!' I shouted back. 'I'm never gonna forget this place.'

We stood there a minute longer, not speaking, feeling the cool mist settle on our faces.

'Come on,' I said eventually, putting my hand on Umer's shoulder. 'The village can't be more than ten minutes from here. We need to warn the Agency before it's too late.'

We set off along the river bank in the direction we'd last spotted houses. We'd gone less than a hundred metres before we discovered a path.

I could smell the village even before I saw it. Food, spices, curry – nothing had ever smelled so good! Our trudging steps began to pick up a little. Umer was leaning forward, like he was being dragged along by his nose. My mouth began to water. We were saved!

The path we were following had grown wide by this point, having joined up with one or two other tracks leading out of the woods. We rounded a corner and there it was, the entrance to the village. Houses, animals and people – real live people!

'We did it,' I said. 'We're safe!'

'Great,' said Umer. 'Let's eat.'

It was a good shout. We hadn't eaten for hours and the food smells were quickly becoming torture. It all looked amazing. Butter chicken, aloo gobi, pakora – all my favourites were cooking away, or piled high on little tables or mats on the ground. We wandered through the marketplace, taking in the mouth-watering smells.

'Humza,' said Umer over the rumbling of our stomachs, 'is it me, or do the people round here dress a bit funny?'

'Yeah, course they do. It's rural Pakistan. What did you expect?'

'Right, I know, but . . . it's more than that,' he continued. 'They look a bit . . . retro.'

'Retro?'

'Yeah, you know, seventies or something. Take that guy,' he said, pointing to a man in flared trousers. 'His clothes, his haircut, his sideburns. He looks like he's going to a fancy-dress party.'

'Exactly. Rural Pakistan. They're like five decades behind us. They won't get fidget spinners until, like, 2050.'

'OK, well, what about that car then?' he said, pointing to the only vehicle around. 'It must be fifty years old.'

'Umer, what part of "rural Pakistan" don't you understand? Everything here's weird and outdated.'

'Fine,' he said in the stubborn voice he puts on when he won't let me tell him what to think. 'But something's not right.' And, as he turned away, his mouth fell open, his eyes grew wide.

'What is it?' I asked.

He pointed. 'How do you explain that then?' he said. I turned round to see what he was talking about. Sitting cross-legged on a little scrap of carpet twenty feet away was a boy.

'Explain wha–' I began, but, before I could finish, my own mouth fell open.

Whoa . . . that ain't possible . . .

Umer didn't need to tell me what he'd been thinking. The second I saw the boy, I knew. He was the spitting image of my uncle, Grandpa. Not now, obviously, but back when he was a kid. The boy looked almost identical to Grandpa in that picture of him and my dad. The one in the marketplace. *This* marketplace!

And this kid didn't just look the same, he was doing magic tricks for a little crowd, just like Grandpa had once told me he used to do as a teenager, right in this spot. But that was back in the . . .

1970s!

'No way,' I gasped.

I looked around me. Seventies clothes. Seventies cars. Not a mobile phone in sight.

It *couldn't be* . . .

Was this kid sitting in front of me really . . . *Grandpa*?

CHAPTER SEVENTEEN

UNCLE TARIQ

I couldn't help staring like an idiot as Umer dragged me across the market square towards the boy on the carpet. Some part of me still couldn't accept the idea. Even though I'd already seen dinosaurs, cavemen and killer robots that day, my brain still refused to admit that Umer and I might have landed back in the 1970s – right in the village my family came from. I just wasn't ready to believe that the kid sitting there, making handkerchiefs disappear, was my uncle.

The closer we got, though, the more and more obvious it became. The boy was speaking in Urdu, which Grandpa never really did with me, but the voice was his. Closer still and I could see that his hairline was already receding a little and patches of grey were visible on his temples. Man, going bald and grey has gotta be tough for a teenager. He couldn't have been fifteen. Dad was right: Grandpa did start looking old early. And it had happened pretty fast apparently. This Grandpa-kid probably only had about three years left before he started looking like a middle-aged accountant with a stress disorder.

When we arrived at the edge of his carpet, he was in the middle of joining three solid metal rings together, before slipping them apart again. He was concentrating hard and didn't look up at us until the trick was done. Umer began to clap, but he was the only one. The rest of the crowd immediately started wandering off into the marketplace. I couldn't move though. I was standing there gawping, mouth wide open like a trout who's just been told he's won the lottery.

The kid on the carpet looked up at us and smiled. '*As-salaam alaikum*,' he said.

'*Wa-alaikum salaam*,' we replied automatically.

'Nice trick,' I added without thinking.

A puzzled look fell across the boy's face. 'You . . . are . . . English?' he asked.

'Yeah, that's right,' I said. 'We're . . . uh . . . on

holiday. But my family come from around here. Real close by, actually.'

'Slow, please,' he said, holding up his hands. 'I do not speak often English. I still learn.'

'Oh, sorry,' I replied, slowing right down. 'My name's Humza. This is Umer.'

'I am Tariq,' he said.

Tariq! Man, this was all just too weird. Of course his name was Tariq – I knew it had to be – but it was still crazy hearing him confirm it. This was him. This was Grandpa. We'd tumbled through a hundred million years that afternoon, and fate had dropped us right here. Right in this very spot.

And that was when something massively obvious dawned on me. Somewhere in this village there was a little kid running about called Mohammed Ali Khan, a kid who would one day grow up, put on a ton of weight, get real angry and become my dad. Just the thought of it knocked all the words out of my head.

Thankfully, Umer filled the silence before it got weird. 'You're really good at magic,' he said, smiling.

'Thank you,' replied Tariq. 'Do you know any tricks? I wish to learn more.'

'No, sorry,' said Umer. 'But Humza knows a couple.'

'Oh!' said Tariq. 'You know magic?'

'A bit,' I mumbled. This was too weird! *He* was the one who'd taught *me*!

'Will you show me?' he asked.

'Uh . . . OK . . . sure,' I said, slipping out the old coin Grandpa had given me to practise with. I'd been practising the hole-in-the-hand trick in bed at night since we'd got here, and I figured I was getting pretty good at it now. But I still hadn't tested it out on anyone.

I held the coin up in one hand for Tariq to see, then began to tap it on the back of my other hand, just like Grandpa had shown me. Once . . . twice . . . then on the third tap the coin appeared to fall right through my hand and into the collection bowl on his mat.

'Oh!' exclaimed Tariq, laughing. 'You have a hole in your hand.'

He reached into the bowl to hand the coin back to me.

'No, that's OK,' I said, smiling at him. 'You keep it.'

'Are you sure?' he asked, looking concerned.

'Yeah, you earned it,' I told him. And somehow it felt right. Sure, it was a special coin and all, the one I'd learned to do my first-ever trick with, but it's not like he wouldn't give it back to me. It would just take him fifty years to get around to it . . . Man, that was too crazy to think about for long!

Tariq looked super happy when he accepted the coin, but his eyes began to widen as he examined it.

'Old ten paise,' he said with a big smile. 'Rare coin. Not made any more. Very special.'

'Well, you should probably hang on to it then,' I told him. 'Might come in real handy one day.'

He grinned as he slipped it into his pocket. I smiled back at him. It was strange, but I didn't expect the sudden wave of emotion. It hit me out of nowhere. The weird connection I had with this person, across decades and continents. Everything we'd been through, and he didn't even know it yet. I could barely get my head round all the things I was feeling.

But it turns out I wasn't the only one having an emotional reaction. Umer suddenly looked like he might cry.

'*Sooo hungrrryyyyy,*' he groaned, drooling over the

fresh rotis being carried past by some market guy.

'Food?' said Tariq. 'You are wanting food?'

Umer's head whipped round. He started nodding like a seal at feeding time.

'Umer!' I said, elbowing him. 'Be cool, man.'

But to be fair my mouth was watering too. It would be a shame for us to starve to death before we'd worked out how to get back home and stop Mr Malik from destroying the Agency.

'Please,' said Tariq, standing up. 'You come with me. Dinner. You come.' Without even waiting for a reply, he scooped his tricks into a little basket, rolled up his carpet and tucked them both under one arm.

'Come, come, come,' he said, then he hurried off towards the edge of the marketplace.

'I guess we follow him,' said Umer.

'I guess so,' I agreed.

And that was how I came to have the weirdest family dinner of my entire life . . .

Dad was staring at me over his little plate of daal and rice. That's right. My dad! My tiny eight-year-old scruffy-looking dad! It was so far beyond weird, they ain't invented a word for it yet. And if they had, it'd be too weird to say out loud. If you tried, your head would just explode from all the weirdness.

'Why's he staring at you like that?' whispered Umer, who was sitting cross-legged beside me on the floor.

'I don't know,' I replied, 'but I can't look away.' I couldn't tell if my dad was angry or curious, or just plain crazy, but he never took his eyes off me, even as he shovelled handfuls of daal and rice into his mouth. We were all sitting round a thick, colourful blanket spread out on the floor. In the centre of it was a stack of steaming dishes, heaped with some of my favourite foods. Everyone was helping themselves to everything. It was like an old family photo come to life.

And everybody was there – my dad, Uncle Tariq, loads of my other aunts and uncles, their parents (my grandparents!) and even their parents' parents (my *great*-grandparents!). It was amazing.

I pulled my eyes away from my dad's weird stare and turned to my grandmother.

'Uh, *shukria*, Mrs Khan,' I said. I didn't remember a lot of Urdu, but I was pretty sure that was 'thank you'. Tariq had been helping to translate everything else.

'You . . . welcome,' replied my grandmother with a big smile. She spoke about as much English as I could speak Urdu, and I could see she was making a real effort. The food was lovely, and she was treating me and Umer just like family, even though I hadn't told them who I really was. I felt a bit surprised by just how good it was to see her. I mean, I didn't really know my grandma; I'd only met her and my grandfather when I was a baby and had been too young to remember it. They never came to England, and they died when I was still pretty little. But she had the nicest face ever. Like a happy prune. I only really knew that face from photos, but it felt so familiar, so much like home, I just wanted to give her a hug. That would have looked weird, though, so instead we just grinned at each other over a huge bowl of daal.

'Eat?' she said, gesturing to the bowl.

'No, thanks. I hate daal,' I replied before I could stop myself. 'Oops . . . uh . . . don't translate that,' I said to Tariq as quickly as I could. 'Just tell her I'm full.'

Tariq explained, and she smiled at me, nodding. Man, that was close. I didn't want to offend my grandma after she'd cooked for us. It's just that daal's my kryptonite. I'd rather eat a foot. Umer on the other hand was already diving in for his third helping.

It was funny, but sitting there with everyone, I suddenly realized it was the happiest I'd been since we'd left England. It felt just like the family dinners we have every weekend (right down to my angry-looking dad staring at me across the blanket like he's about to throw a shoe at my head). Somehow, as lost as I was, I'd found a little bit of home.

And you know what else was bizarre? Even though I'd seen photos of Dad as a kid, I'd never noticed just how much he looked like me. Less handsome, obviously, but the resemblance was there. And, if there had been any doubt remaining that this kid was my dad, it vanished the second he opened his mouth . . .

'You are not as strong as me,' he barked all of a sudden.

The entire rest of the family went quiet at this point, then turned to look at me. Apparently, they wanted to hear my view on the subject. Uncle Tariq was the only one who looked a bit embarrassed.

'Uh . . . *what*?' I replied, a little taken aback.

'Look at your arms! Look at my arms,' he continued. 'You are not as strong as me!'

'Um . . . OK . . .' I replied.

'Please, ignore my little brother,' said Uncle Tariq, blushing a little. 'Mohammed is sometimes showing off.'

'I can lift a dog in each hand and still run,' continued my dad.

'Oh . . .' I replied. 'That's . . . uh . . . weird.'

'*You* cannot do this!' he snapped.

'It's never really come up.'

'You would fail!' he declared, banging his fist down.

'Yeah, you're probably right,' I said with an awkward smile, hoping someone would come to my rescue.

Umer seemed to be concentrating extra hard on his plate all of a sudden. It looked like he was doing his best not to laugh. Everyone else was just staring at me, like they were watching *EastEnders* over dinner. All except Tariq, who had put his face in his hands and was shaking his head back and forth.

'I can jump over a cow,' said my dad, moving on to a new subject.

Again the family waited for my response. *Can you also jump over a cow?* their faces seemed to ask.

'Uh . . . that's great,' I replied. 'Good for you.'

'*You* cannot do this!' he yelled.

'What, jump over a cow?' I said. Then, cos I couldn't help myself, I added, 'Sure, I can jump over a cow. Actually, I can jump over two cows.'

'Liar!' my dad cried. 'You have never jumped over two cows!'

Man, I really should learn to keep my big mouth shut. But, I tell you, there was something about this annoying kid that really wound me up. Still, I was a guest in his home, so best not to let it get out of hand.

'Yup, sorry,' I said, smiling at the furious little goblin. 'You're right. I've never jumped over any cows.'

'I can jump over three cows!' he yelled. 'I can run faster than train, punch hole through tree, sit in fire, eat rock, dig through –' And he would have kept going too if I hadn't interrupted him.

'OK, OK,' I said, holding up my hands. 'I believe you. I can't do any of that stuff. You're the best. You win.'

He stared at me for a moment, like he was working out if I was joking or not. Then a dark cloud came over his face, his brow furrowed, his nostrils flared and he growled like a dog. Without another word, he jumped to his feet and stormed out of the room.

There was a moment's silence before the family went right back to eating and chattering away.

'What was that about?' I asked Tariq.

'Mohammed just wants to impress you,' he replied.

'*Impress* me?' I asked with a laugh. 'He looked

like he wanted to kill me.'

'I am sorry,' said Tariq. 'I am sure he will grow out of this behaviour.'

'Don't count on it,' I replied, shaking my head.

Man, that poor family had no idea what was in store for them. I tell you, that kid sure could use some discipline . . .

CHAPTER EIGHTEEN

ZERO PER CENT

After we'd finished dinner, Tariq took us through to the bedroom he shared with his brothers and sisters, so he could show us some more of his magic tricks. The other kids were off doing their chores, but Tariq had been given permission to entertain us instead.

It was a funny little house. It looked like it had been built at several different times, with new bits made of different materials added on here and there. There was a big family room, which was the one we'd just eaten our dinner in, and that doubled up as the kitchen. Then there was this room, which had half a dozen beds on the floor and not much else. And then there was another room, where my grandparents slept. Apparently, my great-grandparents slept in the main family room when it wasn't being used by everyone else. It was pretty different to how I was used to living, but the house still felt cosy. Still felt like home.

'Now,' said Tariq, pulling a bit of string through his closed fist before holding it up in the air. 'The rope is whole again! See? No cut!'

He was clearly excited about having someone new to perform for, and he was rattling through his act so fast that there was barely time to clap, though Umer kept trying. Me, though – I couldn't concentrate. Now that I'd eaten something, my brain was starting to work properly again. It was beginning to dawn on me how messed up this whole situation really was. With the watch busted, I didn't have a clue how to get back to our own time. All I knew was that, somehow, we had to warn the Agency that Mr Malik was coming to wipe them out . . .

And then it struck me.

'The Agency!' I blurted out.

Umer and Tariq both turned and looked at me, confused.

'Huh?' replied Umer.

'Umer!' I said, grabbing him. 'I know how to do

it! I know how to get us home!'

'Really?' he replied with an excited smile.

'You go home already?' said Tariq, who looked less happy about the news.

'We have to, I'm afraid. We've got something really important to do.'

Tariq nodded and smiled that little smile of his that would one day grow into Grandpa's goofy, toothy, gappy grin.

'Thanks for feeding us though,' I added. 'You probably saved our lives.'

'You are welcome,' he said, looking embarrassed and pleased all at once.

'Can you excuse us for just a second?' I said, getting up. 'We need to discuss our travel plans out in the hall.'

Tariq looked a bit puzzled but nodded. Umer and I headed straight for the little bit of corridor connecting the house's two bedrooms with the living area.

'Have you figured out how to repair the watch?' asked Umer when it was safe to speak.

'Course not,' I replied. 'I'm rubbish at fixing things. I burned down my dad's shed mending the smoke alarm. But I *do* know who *could* fix it.'

'Who?' replied Umer.

'The Agency. They're bound to have some top-level science geeks who can figure it out. It can't be that badly broken.'

'But what if it's not that easy? What if they can't work it out right away and it takes them years?' fretted Umer. 'Will we just have to live here until then?'

'No, that's the best bit. As soon as someone repairs the watch, they can jump in time and get us. Even if it takes them a hundred years to fix it, for us it'll be instant!'

'You mean they'd just . . . appear?'

'Exactly. As soon as we give this watch to the Agency, someone from the future will be able to jump right back to this moment in time and collect us. Good solution, huh?'

'Yeah, that's brilliant. So what happens next?' asked Umer.

'We turn this thing on,' I replied, whipping Grandpa's phone out of my bag. 'Agent Akbar can tell us exactly how to contact the Agency here in the past. Now get ready for some Transformers-level awesomeness.' And, with that, I pressed the phone's OK button.

The screen glowed for just a moment, barely long enough for me to see the battery symbol flashing. Then it went dead. I pressed the OK button again. Nothing. And again – still nothing. This time the screen wasn't coming on at all.

'It still looks kind of rubbish,' said Umer, sounding disappointed.

'The battery,' I groaned. 'It must be dead.'

Man, I wasn't used to keeping a mobile phone charged. I wish I'd thought to plug it in yesterday. This never happened to James Bond.

'OK. It's no big deal,' said Umer. 'We just need to charge it up for a bit. Let's ask Tariq.'

'Yeah,' I agreed. 'He's hardly gonna say no, is he?'

'No,' said Tariq when we joined him back in the bedroom.

'What? Why not?' I replied. 'We only need like two pence worth of electricity! Umer'll give you his shoes to pay for it.'

'No, you do not understand,' said Tariq. 'We have no electricity. In cities, yes. But not here. We are small village.'

'You can't be serious!' I gasped. 'Everyone's got electricity.'

'I am sorry,' he said with a little shrug.

'But . . . what do you do when it gets dark?' Umer asked, sounding a bit desperate.

'We light lamps,' Tariq replied, lifting a small brass oil lamp from the windowsill.

'Lamps? I can't charge my phone with lamps!' I cried.

'Phone?' he replied, sounding confused.

'Yeah. Don't worry about that,' I said, already starting to think about how we could get to the city to find somewhere with a plug socket.

'There is one option, perhaps,' said Tariq. 'But it is . . . complicated.'

'What is it?' I asked.

'There is a family in the village. Rich family. They have their own motor car.'

'Motor car?' asked Umer, confused. 'You think they'll drive us into town?'

'No, not to drive,' said Tariq, shaking his head. 'For electricity.'

'I don't understand,' I replied. 'I thought you said no one here had electricity?'

'The car,' explained Tariq. 'Car is electricity. Car is battery.'

'The car is a *battery*?' I asked, totally baffled

by this point.

'Yes,' said Tariq with a nod. 'It is . . . generator.'

Now, I didn't know a lot about cars or batteries, or any of that stuff, but I did know that my mum charged her phone every time we drove anywhere in her Micra. And somehow this kid from the 1970s, who'd never owned a car, never charged a phone, probably never even plugged anything in, had come up with the answer. I'd never understood until that moment just how brilliant my uncle really was.

'That's it!' I said. 'That's how we'll do it! Can we go and see them now?'

'Now?' said Tariq, sounding a little surprised.

He looked out of the window and up into the sky. He thought for a moment, then nodded.

'Yes. Now is good,' he declared.

'Great,' I said, jumping up. 'Let's go!'

'There is one problem,' added Tariq.

'What problem?' asked Umer.

'They will not give you electricity. Ever.'

'What? Why not?' I asked.

'They are not nice people.'

'Oh . . .' I replied. 'Well . . . in that case, we'll just have to take it.'

★

We said our goodbyes to everyone except Dad, who hadn't come back since his disappearing act at dinner. I even got a hug from Grandma as I left. I'll never forget how she smelled or how soft her cheek was against mine. (But if you tell anyone I said that, I'll make you eat my PE kit.)

'Bye, guys!' I said, waving back at everyone in the living room.

'*Byeeeee!*' they all cheered, then burst out laughing at their own English.

I had a big grin on my face as I pushed open the front door and stepped out into the evening light. My smile lasted just long enough for a bucket of filthy water to crash down on top of me. In an instant, I was drenched. The bucket bounced off my head and landed at my feet in the dirt. Even without the shriek of laughter that followed, it wouldn't have taken a genius to work out who was responsible.

'Ha ha!' squealed my little dad, who was hopping about by a run-down old barn ten metres away. He bent over double, his hands on his knees, then rose up again, pointing at us and wailing with laughter.

'Ow,' I said, rubbing the bruise under my hat where the bucket had hit me.

'You are wet!' shouted my tiny dad. 'You are very, very wet!'

Umer and Tariq were standing behind me in the doorway, wide-eyed. 'I am so sorry,' said Tariq, stepping out of the house.

'It's not your fault,' I said through gritted teeth. Man, my dad was the worst! I'd always thought I might have got on with him when he was a kid. I'd figured that, before the world crushed all the joy out of him, Dad might have been quite fun. But instead, now I'd met him, I just wanted to roll him up in a carpet and drop him off a waterfall. And I knew just where to find one . . .

As I stepped into the yard, Dad began to back off, clearly planning to run if I came near him. If it wasn't already so close to sunset, I'd have chased him down and stuffed him inside his own bucket. But there wasn't time. We had to get to that car. So, with a clenched jaw and a dripping hat, I marched from the house towards the forest path, ignoring the sound of my dad's hysterical laughter and the squelching of my shoes.

'I hate that kid,' I muttered under my breath as we made our way into the undergrowth. 'I tell you, he seriously needs some discipline.' As I said it, there was a snigger from behind me. This time though, the laughter wasn't coming from my dad.

'What's so funny?' I snapped, turning to face Umer.

He was clearly doing his best to hold it in and was failing pretty miserably.

'You think this is amusing?' I said, gesturing to my wet clothes.

'No,' he said, breaking out in a huge grin.

'You *do*!' I shouted.

'I'm not laughing cos you're soaked,' he said. 'I'm laughing cos it's you.'

'What you talking about? Course it's me! Who else would it be?'

'No, I mean, *he's* you! He's just like you and you can't see it.'

'What? No, he ain't. He's just some annoying kid who needs discipline.'

Umer cracked up again.

'Stop laughing!' I yelled.

'Pulling pranks, making stuff up, telling everyone he's amazing?' said Umer. 'Yeah, you're right. He's nothing like you.'

'Shut up, Umer! You don't know what you're

talking about,' I snapped, but he'd lost it now and couldn't stop.

'Right, you know what?' I told him. 'I don't even want to talk to you until we're back in the twenty-first century!'

CHAPTER NINETEEN
THE HEIST

You ever see any of them Ocean's Eleven movies? Big glamorous casino heists in Las Vegas? Well, this was the opposite of that. Three Pakistani kids throw together a plan to rob twopence worth of electricity from some guy's car. Hollywood ain't gonna be ringin' anytime soon.

The car was parked exactly where Tariq said it would be, outside a large house on the other side of the village. It was the same car I'd spotted in the marketplace that afternoon – the seventies-looking one that had seemed so outdated. Of course, now I realized, it was actually brand new.

As we watched from the bushes at the edge of the forest, a man came out of the house, opened the driver's door and turned on the ignition. The engine began to purr. He closed the door again, then turned and followed a cable that ran from under the car's bonnet, along the ground and over to a wooden box on a nearby table. Then he lifted the lid of the box and flicked a switch. There was a small spark and a tiny crackle, then, in an instant, two or three light bulbs burst into life inside the house. The man turned and walked back inside.

'They use car battery to power lights,' said Tariq. 'One or two hours each night.'

'Tariq,' I whispered to him, 'you're a genius.'

He smiled a big smile.

'So, what's the plan?' said Umer. 'Do we just walk up and plug the phone in?'

'I guess so,' I said. 'He probably won't be back anytime soon. Half an hour should be enough. Come on.'

I jumped up and hurried over towards the car. The others followed. At the table, I popped my bag down and fished out the phone and charger. Tariq stared at it wide-eyed but said nothing. I lifted the lid of the little wooden box and peered in.

'What the . . .?' I said, staring down at the chaos inside. 'The hell is this?'

It was a handmade mess of wires and fuses and

hunks of metal. I had been expecting an extension cord with a bunch of plug sockets. Instead it looked like a robot had exploded.

'This ain't a plug,' I said.

'No?' replied Tariq, sounding concerned.

'Uh-uh. I haven't got a clue what this thing is.'

'Alternator,' came a small voice from behind us.

Even though the voice was soft, we all jumped as if a gunshot had gone off. We spun round to see a kid of seven or eight a few feet away, close to the door the man had disappeared through. He had big wide eyes and a round bald head. He was

pretty small and didn't look like much of a threat. But, on the other hand, he *did* appear to be carrying a cricket bat.

'It is an alternator,' he repeated.

'Oh . . . right,' I replied. I had no idea what an alternator was. 'So . . . you speak English?'

He nodded.

'His name is Amir,' whispered Tariq. 'I have only seen him rarely. His father owns this car.'

'We were just . . .' I began. 'We were hoping we might borrow a bit of your dad's electricity. Would you be able to help us?'

He stared at us but said nothing.

'I want to plug this in,' I said, holding up the phone charger. 'See? I just can't work out how.'

Again, he only stared. I realized he mustn't understand at all. This really wasn't going well.

'You play cricket with me?' he said after a moment, holding up the bat along with a ball he was clutching in his other hand.

'Uh . . . no, sorry,' I replied. 'We ain't really got time for cricket right now. But we do need to get some electricity. Do you know what *electricity* is?'

'I can fix,' he said.

'Huh?' I replied, not quite believing it. 'Really?'

'I will fix,' he nodded. 'And *you* will play cricket.'

'Seriously? Cricket?' I said, grimacing. 'How about if you just fix it for us and we *don't* play cricket?'

But Amir didn't seem to be listening. He walked straight up, took the charger out of my hand and began to connect it up to some wires in the box. He seemed pretty confident as he wrapped the exposed ends of the cables round the plug's prongs. We all watched quietly as he worked. In under a minute, he was done. He flicked a switch, there was a moment's pause, and then the light on the phone's screen popped on. The charging icon appeared.

'You did it!' I gasped.

'Amazing!' said Umer.

'Thank you, Amir,' said Tariq with a warm smile.

But Amir didn't smile back.

'Now cricket,' he replied. The kid was good. He had us just where he wanted us. There was no getting out of it. It looked like we were going to be playing cricket with him.

'All right, Amir,' I said, reaching over and taking the ball from where he'd placed it on the table while he worked. 'We'll play with you for as long as it takes to charge up. OK?'

He grinned and picked up his bat. The sun had dipped beneath the trees now, and the sky was red and pink and orange. I didn't think we'd get all that much play in before it was too dark to see anything, but even twenty minutes would do the trick.

And that's how I came to play cricket in a small forest clearing beneath a burning red sky in Pakistan, with my best friend, my uncle and a funny little bald kid named Amir.

Once it was too dark to play, and we'd nearly lost the ball in the trees for the fifth time, I checked on the phone. Thirty-six per cent. That'd do it. Amir had a massive grin on his face as he charged back from the undergrowth with the ball in his hands. It was nice that he'd had a good time. He seemed like a pretty lonely kid.

'Thanks, Amir,' I said as I disconnected the phone from its charger. 'You're a lifesaver.'

'You will come and play cricket with me again tomorrow?' he asked.

'Ah, man, I'm sorry,' I replied. 'We can't. We've got to get home.'

A glower fell across his face, half disappointed, half angry.

'Go then,' he snapped.

'Hey, come on, Amir,' I said, smiling at him. 'Don't be angry.'

'Go!' he yelled. 'Or I will call my father.' The kid was furious. It looked like I'd really hurt his feelings.

'We'd play longer if we could,' said Umer. 'We just have to get home.'

'Go!' he shouted, then he turned towards the house and yelled, 'Abu-jee!'

'We had better run,' said Tariq. 'His father is . . . strict.'

It was weird. I felt bad for this kid who'd helped us – and yet sort of annoyed with him too. But what could I do? We couldn't stick around. I shoved the phone into my bag and we ran off into the forest.

CHAPTER TWENTY

DOUBLE-O-TROUBLE

'Do not blame Amir,' said Tariq as we wandered back along the path. 'He is kept from playing with other children in the village.'

'What, by his dad?' I asked.

'Mmm.' Tariq nodded. 'His father believes they are better than the rest of us because of their wealth. One day, unfortunately, Amir will be like him.'

'That's a shame,' replied Umer. 'He seemed like a nice kid.'

And Umer was right. It was a shame. Before Amir had flipped out, I'd kinda liked him too. But it can't be easy, living out here in the middle of nowhere when your dad won't let you make friends. I'd be frustrated too.

But then I reminded myself: this was all ancient

history. We'd travelled through time and whatever that kid's dad had done to him had nothing to do with us – it had happened over forty years ago. All we had to worry about was getting back to the present and stopping Mr Malik. And now that the phone was up and running again, I'd be able to ask AI Akbar how to make contact with the Agency here in the 70s. Once that was done, we'd be on our way home.

Tariq's house and Amir's house were at opposite ends of the village and the route took us right back into the heart of the woods. We walked through the darkness, listening to the sounds of the forest at night. Now that we had Tariq as a guide, I wasn't so afraid of being eaten by bears or getting lost and starving to death. It was actually pretty amazing being in the forest after dark.

It was strange to think that, if my mum and dad hadn't decided to move to England before I was born, then this might have been my home. These woods would have been as familiar to me as they were to Tariq, who was currently guiding us along an invisible path without any effort at all.

As we walked, I began to think about my mum's childhood, here in Pakistan. It was so strange to think of her, far away on the other side of the country, probably asleep in her own bed, in her own house, in her own little village. Mohammed and Nausheen, my dad and mum, wouldn't meet for years and years, not until they were all grown up. I suddenly felt a pang of sadness that I wasn't going to get to see her too. I bet she'd be easier to get on with than my dad. Then again, an elephant with a migraine would be easier to get along with than my dad.

As we stepped out of the woods and into the clearing, there in front of us was the family house, its white walls glowing in the moonlight.

'Thanks for helping us with that,' I said to Tariq as we walked through the yard. 'For everything, actually. You've been amazing.'

'My pleasure,' he replied with a grin. 'Now that you have what you need, where will you go?'

Umer and I looked at each other. We needed somewhere to crash while we put our plan into action, and I don't think either of us was keen on spending the night in the forest.

'Well, actually, the thing is . . .' I began, 'we don't really have anywhere –'

'Do not worry,' said Tariq, cutting me off.

'I know the perfect place for you.'

'Wow, thanks, man,' I said with a huge smile.

Turned out 'perfect' might have been a *bit* of an exaggeration . . .

You ever look a goat in the eye? It's freaky. They've got these weird rectangular pupils that make them look totally evil. In fact, the only thing more evil than a goat's eyes is its smell. And our new 'bedroom' had plenty of both.

'Is this where your goats live?' asked Umer as we peered into the little barn Tariq had led us to.

Barely visible at the far end of the battered old shack, half a dozen goats stared back at us, their scary-looking pupils glinting in the lamplight.

'Indeed,' replied Tariq, hanging the oil lamp on a hook by the door. 'You may stay as long as you wish.'

'Right. And where are the goats gonna stay?' I asked.

'They will remain here also,' replied Tariq, looking confused.

'Yeah, I was afraid you might say that.'

'Thanks, Tariq,' said Umer, who was better at being polite than me. 'This'll be great.'

'Uh . . . yeah, man. Thanks,' I added, giving him the closest thing to a smile I could manage.

'You are welcome,' replied Tariq. 'I must return home. My family will wonder what has happened to me.'

'Night, Gramp– I mean, Tariq,' I stuttered, barely covering my mistake. Man, I was getting tired. Tariq didn't seem to notice though. He nodded a quick goodbye, then hurried off towards the house.

Everything was silent for a moment. Eerily silent. Umer and I turned our heads very slowly towards the back of the barn. It's a strange feeling to have six quiet goats staring at you.

'Evening,' I said to the goats.

The goats didn't reply. They just stared at us with those evil goat eyes. Damn, those guys were creepy.

'All right,' I said, whipping out the phone. 'Let's find out how we get home.'

The bright green light from the facial-recognition scanner filled the barn.

'Whoa . . .' gasped Umer as the whole device burst into life. It whirred and clicked as it transformed from brick to futuristic tablet. The glow from the screen was reflected in a dozen rectangular pupils in the darkness. Someone bleated (possibly Umer).

When the transformation was complete, a face appeared on the screen.

'Greetings, Agent Badman,' said the AI simulation of Agent Akbar. 'Good evening, Umer.'

'*Whoa* . . .' breathed Umer, gawping at the screen. 'How does he know my name?'

'I am familiar with all the key figures in the recent alien invasion,' replied AI Akbar. 'You did an excellent job of saving the world.'

'Oh . . . thanks,' said Umer, blushing a little and beaming with pride.

'How is your mission in Pakistan proceeding?' asked the simulation.

'So . . . uh . . . how can I put this?' I replied. 'We may have accidentally gone back in time a bit.'

'*Back in time?*' said AI Akbar, sounding as surprised as a computer simulation of a guy's head can sound.

'It's quite a long story,' I told him, 'but we've only got thirty per cent battery, so no interruptions.'

'Please continue,' replied AI Akbar.

So I did. I explained about Mr Malik and how the Agency had been right about him all along. He *had* been working on powerful inventions at the school. And now, because Umer and I had stuck our noses in, he was planning to wipe out the Agency once and for all. I described the secret underground lab we'd discovered, and the pocket watch we'd 'borrowed' for research purposes. I explained how, when we'd dropped it, we'd been blasted back in time – same place, wrong decade – and that now we were stuck.

When I was all done, everyone was silent, even the goats. It was the first time I'd seen the simulation look totally baffled – it didn't fill me with confidence.

'Fascinating . . .' said AI Akbar eventually. 'I do not believe I am programmed to help with this specific eventuality.'

'Don't worry about that,' I told him. 'We've already got a plan. We just need help finding a scientist who can fix the watch and get us home.'

'I'm afraid,' began the simulation, 'here in the 1970s, the available technology is considerably less advanced than our own. Even if you were able to locate a scientist, they would be unlikely to know how to repair such a device –'

'Yeah, but that's the clever bit,' I interrupted. 'It doesn't matter if they can't fix it straight away. As long as I can get it to the Agency, you guys can take as much time as you need to figure it out. And, once you've figured it out, you just need to come back here and rescue us. Brilliant, huh?'

'It is an excellent plan,' replied AI Akbar. 'But there is one small problem.'

'What?'

'There is no Agency here for you to contact. They do not yet exist.'

'*WHAT?*' cried Umer and I at the same time.

'At this point in history,' continued the simulation, 'the Agency has not even been founded. I am afraid you are completely on your own.'

CHAPTER TWENTY-ONE
MAGIC LESSONS

I ain't gonna pretend it was a good night's sleep. Finding out there was no Agency there to help us would have been bad enough on its own. But there ain't nothing as terrifying as being woken up at three in the morning by a goat who wants a cuddle. And, when I wasn't being spooned by lonely goats, I was having nightmares about slipping further back in time until the whole world disappeared from under my feet. But, as rubbish as all of that was, none of it compared to our wake-up call . . .

'*Aarghhh!*' I spluttered as the tidal wave of dirty water crashed down on my head. At first, I didn't have a clue what was going on – I wasn't even sure where I was. But the moment I heard the laughter, I knew.

Dad! I shook the water out of my eyes and looked up. He was standing in the doorway, holding an empty bucket, creasing up at how incredibly funny he was.

'You little punk!' I shouted. 'Stop doing that!'

'I've changed my mind,' grumbled Umer, looking wet and miserable. 'He is worse than you.'

'See! I told you he was!'

The goats clearly weren't happy either and were bleating like crazy. It must have been a hell of a racket, because a moment later we heard the front door to the house bang open and the sound of Tariq's voice in the yard. He was already yelling something in Urdu as he charged into the barn. My miniature dad was laughing his head off as he dodged this way and that to avoid his big brother's attempts to grab hold of him. Tariq eventually managed to chase Dad through the door and out into the yard.

A moment later, Tariq returned with an embarrassed look on his face.

'I am so very sorry,' he said.

'Has no one in Pakistan ever heard of the naughty step?' I grumbled. 'Because that kid needs to spend about eight years sitting on it!'

It took Umer less than three seconds to start laughing. Sitting there in the mud, dripping wet, surrounded by a bunch of freaked-out goats, I really didn't want to join in. But, when I looked at Umer's big round grinning face, I couldn't help it. And once Tariq realized we weren't upset, he burst out laughing too. The only ones not amused were the goats. I guess they didn't get it. Stupid goats.

'What are we gonna do now?' asked Umer a little while later, when we had dried off in the morning sun.

'I don't know, man,' I replied. 'Without the Agency, we're completely stuck. We might just have to get used to living in that barn.'

'No way!' replied Umer. 'One of those goats stuck his tongue in my ear last night. It was the most disgusting thing I've ever felt.'

'Are you not able to go home as planned?' asked Tariq, who'd just returned from the house with some naan for us to eat.

'It's OK,' I told him. 'I'm sure we'll figure something out.'

He stared at me, his face full of concern, then he slipped a hand into his pocket.

'Here,' he said, and passed me something. I opened my hand to discover he'd given me back the coin — the one I'd said he could keep when we'd first met in the marketplace. 'I think you will need this now,' he said with a smile.

'No, man,' I replied. 'I told you: that's for you to keep. I *want* you to have it.'

'But if you are stuck here you will need money. This is all I have.'

Ah, man. My uncle was a good guy. And he wasn't wrong: whatever little he had, we had even less than him. But a bit of spare change was hardly gonna keep us from starving to death. And, in my heart, I knew he should have it — he needed that coin if he was going to give it to me one day in the future.

'Seriously,' I said to Tariq, holding out the coin to him. 'It's yours. You're gonna need it for your coin tricks.'

'Coin tricks?' he replied, sounding puzzled. 'I do not know any coin tricks.'

'Yeah, you do. What about the one I showed you earlier? The hole-in-the-hand trick?'

'I do not know how it is done,' said Tariq with a little shrug. 'Will you teach me?'

'Course I will,' I said with a grin. 'You'd do the same for me.'

I showed him the trick one more time, before revealing the secret of how it was performed. He wore a look of total concentration as he watched me go through the steps involved. Once he understood how it was done, he couldn't wait to give it a go himself. Within minutes, he was already starting to master it. He picked it up even quicker than I did.

'I will show this trick at school,' he said, grinning at the little coin between his fingers.

'School? When's that?' I asked.

'Right now,' he replied. 'I will be late if I do not leave soon.'

I hadn't even thought about these guys going to school, but I guess they had to have been learning English somewhere.

'Normally I leave my tricks at home,' he added with a big smile. 'But this fits right in my pocket.' He slipped the coin into his trousers and grabbed his books, before hurrying off towards the woods. Umer and I stood in the yard and watched him disappear down the forest path.

'I'm confused,' said Umer, once Tariq was out of sight.

'Why, what's up?' I replied.

'That trick you were just doing – didn't your uncle teach you that one?'

'Yeah. So what?'

'Right. But . . . didn't you just teach it to your uncle?'

'Yeah,' I replied, like it was obvious. 'And now that he knows it, he'll be able to show me one day.'

'Uh-huh. And you taught him with the same

coin he gave to you?'

'Yeah.'

'Which you've now given to him?'

'Exactly. So one day he can give it back to me and teach me to do magic tricks.'

'Like the trick you just taught him?'

'Uh-huh.'

'And who taught it to you?'

'He did.'

'And who taught it to him?'

'I did.'

'And who taught you?'

'He . . .' I began, but the words dried up in my mouth. Umer had made his point. Actually, he'd made it about six times, but I guess I hadn't quite woken up yet, because it took that long for it to click. If Grandpa and I had taught each other how to do it, where had the trick come from in the first place? Not to mention the coin.

'It's a paradox,' said Umer.

'A what?'

'A paradox,' Umer repeated. 'That's when something's impossible but it still happens. It can't exist for one reason, but it has to for another.'

'How the hell do you know a word that I don't?'

I spluttered. 'You're just as bad at school as I am.'

'From my auntie. She always says her marriage is a paradox. Living with Uncle Raj makes her want to kill him. But, if he died, she says *her* life wouldn't be worth living.'

'That just sounds like a marriage.'

'Yeah, but this thing with the coin trick is a paradox for sure. He taught you something, then you went back in time and taught him the same thing. That's impossible.'

'Well, yeah, but . . . it happened,' I replied.

'Exactly. And *that's* the paradox. Same with the coin. Where'd it come from in the first place?'

'Huh . . . things get weird when you start messing about with time,' I said, shaking my head. 'If you ever see me about to nick another time-travel device, remind me not to bother.'

'*Or*,' said Umer, smiling, 'you could just use it to go back in time and remind yourself.'

'Urgh . . . More paradoxes!' I said, and I began to laugh – but not for long. All of a sudden, my eyes burst wide open. That was it! That was the answer!

'What's wrong?' asked Umer, who'd noticed the look on my face.

The idea slotted together so perfectly in my head

that something between my ears actually clicked.

'Umer!' I yelled. 'I know how to get us home!'

'How?' he gasped.

'Paradoxes! We need more paradoxes!'

CHAPTER TWENTY-TWO
THE LETTER

Fifteen minutes later, we were sitting in the little clearing by the waterfall. Now that the whole family had woken up, I figured we should get away from the house before opening up the phone. This was the perfect spot to offer a bit of privacy.

'Hello, Agent Badman,' said the simulation as it appeared on the screen.

'Wagwan, Akbar?' I replied. 'I got a question for you.'

'Go right ahead,' said AI Akbar.

'When was the first-ever meeting of the Agency?'

'That information is classified,' said the simulation.

'Ah, go on, you can tell me. I ain't gonna tell no one,' I replied.

'The Agency's origins are one of their most carefully guarded secrets,' replied AI Akbar. 'Only the highest-ranking agents are privy to that information.'

'Ha.' I laughed. 'I knew it!'

'Knew what?' asked Umer.

'It's us!' I cried. 'We're the secret!'

'Eh?' said Umer, looking baffled. 'What are you talking about?'

'*We* started the Agency! You and me!'

'What?'

'Tell me I'm wrong, Akbar!' I said to the phone. 'Tell me it ain't us who started the Agency.'

AI Akbar didn't so much as blink. He just stared at me, frozen.

'See! That's why it's such a big secret. It's too wild to tell anyone. They can't even let their agents know! It was you and me all along, Umer! We started the Agency. Or at least we're about to.'

'What are you talking about, Humza? How can we be the ones who start the Agency? We're just a couple of kids.'

'Look, I can't explain it, but I *know* that's what happens. I'm sure of it. We need the Agency to get us home, right? There is no Agency yet. So we create one. Boom! And the second we do it, the second it's official, the future Agency can jump back and rescue us. It's genius!'

'It's ridiculous,' replied Umer.

'Yeah? What part of our lives isn't ridiculous? Fighting aliens, becoming secret agents, going back in time? And that's just the last few months! If you ask me, this is pretty standard.'

'All right, so, even if you are right, how are two twelve-year-olds meant to set up a top-secret intelligence agency in a village in Pakistan in the 1970s?'

'Well, I was thinking about that on the way here,' I replied. 'I reckon all we actually need to do is hold a meeting.'

'A meeting?'

'Yeah, we just need to make it official. Make sure a record is made of the exact time and date, so they know when to come back and rescue us.'

'What, so, just a meeting between the two of us? Like, right now?'

'No, see, that's the important bit. Someone has to stay here and take over the running of the organization, so we can go home and get on with our lives. We need to recruit our first spy. Someone smart enough to be able to pull it off!'

'Who are we gonna get to do that?' asked Umer.

I stared at him, waiting for the penny to drop. It must have been a pretty deep well, though, cos that penny just kept on falling.

'Who do you think, man?' I eventually said.

'Um . . . Imran Khan?'

'No! Uncle Tariq! Grandpa!'

'Oh yeah, that makes more sense.'

'He told me that the Agency recruited him when he was a teenager,' I said. 'This must be how it happened. We just need to invite him to attend a top-secret meeting. Then, once he shows up, we'll explain the whole thing and tell him about how to rescue us in the future.'

'What if he thinks it's a joke?' asked Umer.

'He won't. Somehow he doesn't. He listens. He becomes a spy and everything that's going to happen happens. Cos, if it didn't happen, we wouldn't be stood here right now, would we?'

'You'd better be right about this, Humza.'

'If I ain't, may I starve to death in a forest in Pakistan,' I replied with a grin.

I don't think Umer liked my joke.

★

An hour later, using a bit of pencil we'd found at the marketplace and some paper we'd fished out of a puddle, we began to draft Tariq's invite to the Agency. I figured a letter from a mysterious agency might help make him take the offer seriously – for a bit, at least. Hopefully long enough to get him into the cave behind the waterfall. After that, I was just going to have to convince him. But that's OK, I'm good at convincing people of stuff. I once convinced Umer that it was 'come as your mum' day at school. He showed up wearing a bright pink dress he'd nicked from his mum's wardrobe. It was amazing. He wasn't even angry when he realized; he had a great time. Turns out Umer kind of suits a shalwar kameez.

Anyway, while I stood over him, dictating what I wanted the letter to say, Umer began writing:

> Dear Mr Khan,
> We are <u>the Agency</u>. We have been
> watching you. We believe that you
> would make a most excellent spy. This
> is your <u>destiny</u>. Come and meet us in
> the cave behind the <u>waterfall</u>. Tonight
> at <u>sundown</u>. This will change your
> life <u>forever</u>.
> Lots of love,
> The Agency
> P.S. <u>Don't</u> tell no one.

'What do you reckon?' I asked once it was finished. 'Did we underline too many words?'

'No,' replied Umer. 'I think that's the perfect amount of underlining.'

'Good. Then let's go make history, bro.'

There was no one around when we got back to the house. We peered in through the window and listened for movement. Nothing. I tried the front door. It was unlocked. We just needed to get in and out as quickly as we could. Deliver the letter and run.

We snuck down the hall towards the kids' bedroom. Still no one around. I peered in through the doorway. The room was empty. In one corner, I spotted Tariq's basket of tricks.

We sprinted over and slipped the letter inside, right on top. When he got home from school and saw it, he'd come straight to the waterfall, I was sure of it. The plan was genius. Nothing could possibly go wrong.

CHAPTER TWENTY-THREE

THE FIRST AGENCY MEETING

It was a little before sunset when we arrived at the cave, so we had some time to kill.

'Wanna play I spy?' suggested Umer.

'No,' I replied. 'I spy's the worst game ever.'

'I spy with my little eye something beginning with C,' said Umer, ignoring me.

'Is it *cave*?' I asked him. (Damn it, I just couldn't help myself!)

'Yeah!' said Umer with an excited grin. 'Your go!'

'How can I go? There's nothing but cave in here. You took the only option!'

'Fine, I'll go again then,' replied Umer before I could stop him. 'I spy with my little eye something beginning with . . .' His face froze.

'Beginning with what?' I sighed.

'D,' he said, pointing towards the mouth of the cave. I turned to see what he was looking at.

'Oh, man,' I groaned.

'You lie!' shouted my tiny dad, who was standing in the entrance, holding up the letter. 'You think this is joke?'

'What the hell are you doing here?' I yelled. 'That ain't your letter!'

'Mr Khan!' he shouted, pointing to the note. 'Me! Mr Khan!'

'No, not you!' I shouted back. 'Not your basket, not your letter! You shouldn't go through your brother's things!' I marched straight over to him and snatched the letter out of his hand.

'Hey!' shouted tiny Dad, trying to snatch it back.

'No!' I yelled, grabbing him by the scruff of his neck and pulling him away. 'You've always told me you had discipline when you were a kid, but you're a little animal. What happened to all the sports you used to win? All the bears you used to beat up? Why aren't you out there playing cricket or something?'

He stopped struggling for a second and looked

up at me. That had caught his attention.

'What, so you *do* like cricket then?' I asked.

He shrugged, not willing to give anything away. An idea began to form as I looked down into those big, wild eyes. I realized I might just have a way of distracting this little monster until we could get the hell out of town.

'Umer, wait here until I get back,' I said, shoving the letter into my pocket.

'Where are you taking me?' demanded my dad as I began marching him towards the mouth of the cave.

'Relax,' I told him. 'You're about to make a new friend.'

'Hey, Amir!' I shouted from the little clearing outside his house. 'Where are you?' I still had my tiny dad by the collar so he couldn't run away, but I reckoned he was curious now anyway. He wasn't struggling at all.

A moment later, Amir looked out from the doorway of the house. 'Hello,' he said without a smile.

'Amir, this is Mohammed,' I told him. 'He's your new friend. He's going to play cricket with you. He loves cricket more than anything in the world; he just doesn't know it yet. So you're going to teach him, OK?'

Amir was quiet a moment. 'OK,' he said eventually.

'Good,' I replied. 'And, as for you,' I continued, turning to my dad, 'I want you to be nice to Amir. No shouting. No throwing water at him. No acting like an animal. You never know, you might just end up with a friend to play with.'

Little Dad just stared at me, full of suspicion.

'Right, go play,' I said, pushing him towards Amir. 'And don't follow me. I don't want to see you again for at least forty years!'

Shaking my head, I marched off into the woods in the direction of the family house. It was time to deliver Tariq's letter. Again!

After dropping off the note, I sprinted back to the waterfall. The sun had almost totally disappeared behind the horizon by the time I got up to the cave. With Dad taken care of, I felt pretty sure that this time everything would go to plan.

'Should we hide behind those rocks?' asked Umer, pointing further into the cave.

'Eh? What for?' I replied.

'You know, so we don't startle him when he comes in,' said Umer, shrugging.

'You think it'll startle him less if we jump out from behind some rocks?'

'I don't know. Maybe,' replied Umer. 'I was just trying to help.'

'I think it'll be OK, man. Tariq knows us. He might think we're kidding at first, but that's where this comes in.' I pulled out the mobile. 'He'll have to believe us once he's seen what this thing can do.'

Outside, the sky was filled with colour. The sun had vanished behind the hills and the pinks and oranges of its last rays poured in through the gushing water, filling the cave with a strange, unreal light.

The colours were only just beginning to fade when a figure stepped in from the path. Tariq looked pretty confused when he saw us.

'Hey, Tariq,' I said. 'I see you got the letter.'

In one hand he was holding the piece of paper and in the other a small oil lamp, its flame flickering in the breeze.

'This is a joke?' he asked, holding out the letter.

'No,' I said, shaking my head. 'It's important.

Really important. We're gonna have to tell you something and it's gonna sound totally crazy. But I swear it's all true – and we can prove it.'

He stood there for a moment, frozen, unsure. 'OK,' he said eventually. 'Tell me.'

It must have taken half an hour to go through everything. We explained where we came from in the future, and about how the Agency had sent us to Pakistan to watch Mr Malik. About how he'd cornered us and sworn to get his revenge. We told Tariq about finding the time-travelling pocket watch and how we'd found ourselves back here by mistake.

Tariq listened in silence, not giving anything away. I had no idea whether he believed us or not.

I just had to keep going. I told him about how important the Agency was going to be in his life. I explained my plan to get us home and that it could only work with his help. I told him everything. Well, everything except for who he was to me. I still don't know why, but I left that one detail out.

When I had finished explaining, Tariq was silent. He stared at me. He stared at Umer.

'Prove,' he said eventually.

'Huh?' I replied.

'You say you can prove this. So prove.'

'OK,' I told him. 'We've got something with us from the future. If you don't believe us after this, I don't think you ever will.'

I lifted the phone and clicked OK. The facial scanner flashed its bright light, causing Tariq to jump back. And then the transformation process began. That alone would probably have been enough to convince him. But the moment the face of Agent Akbar appeared on the screen and greeted us, I knew we had him.

'Hello, Agent Badman. Hello, Umer,' said the simulation before looking over at Tariq. 'Ah,

Agent Grandpa. Good to see you again.'

'What?' gasped Tariq.

'Uh, yeah, just ignore the whole "Grandpa" thing,' I told him. 'That'll make sense in a few years' time.'

'How is this possible?' Tariq said, craning round to look beneath the tablet. 'This is magic?'

'No, not magic,' I replied with a grin. 'Technology. There's gonna be some incredible changes over your lifetime, trust me.'

'I do trust you,' he replied, wide-eyed. 'You are from the future.'

'So you'll do it then?' I asked. 'You'll join the Agency?'

Tariq nodded.

'I will,' he said.

FLASH!

It happened in an instant. Even faster than I'd thought possible. The moment he spoke, the moment he agreed, there was a flash of blue–white light that filled the cave. A ball of lightning burst into existence right in front of us. It pulsed and sparked; it fizzed and crackled with energy. This was it! The Agency had got our message and come back to rescue us. I couldn't believe how well the plan had worked. We were saved! And then a figure stepped out of the glowing sphere. But it wasn't Agent Akbar. It wasn't an agent at all. Something had gone very badly wrong.

'Well, well, well,' said Mr Malik with a thin smile. 'What an unexpected treat.'

CHAPTER TWENTY-FOUR
THE FALL

The ball of blue–white light that Mr Malik had emerged from vanished behind him as he stepped into the cave.

'I had figured you two were dead,' he said to Umer and me, a look of intense curiosity on his face. 'Or, at the very least, that you'd become hopelessly lost somewhere in time. I never thought for a moment I might find you at the first meeting of the . . .'

He stopped in his tracks. The words hung on his lips. His eyes thinned. He was working it out. It can't have taken him much more than a second to put it all together. Damn, this guy was annoyingly smart.

'You . . .' he began. '*You* founded the Agency.

You wound up here and needed a way to get home – so you created it!' He sounded almost impressed for a moment, then he threw his head back and laughed. 'Why, my dear boys, you're not nearly as stupid as you appear.'

I couldn't speak. Umer was frozen to the spot. Tariq looked as scared as he did confused.

'It's actually rather brilliant,' continued Mr Malik. 'Leave a message with the first agent so that, one day, the rest might return and rescue you.' As he spoke, he turned and studied Tariq. 'Unfortunately,' he went on. 'Your precious Agency will never possess the technology required to travel back here. It demands a level of comprehension laughably beyond them. For me, however, it was only a matter of time. Once you stole my watch, I simply set about building a replacement.'

And, as he said it, he held something up. It glinted in the lamplight. I hadn't spotted it until that second. He was holding a brand-new pocket watch! It was identical to the first. He'd rebuilt it from scratch.

'But . . . how did you find out?' I asked. 'About the meeting? No one's meant to know. It's top secret.'

'You're not serious, are you?' he replied through a smirk. 'I designed the Agency's entire encryption system. I know more about their deepest secrets than they do. Admittedly, there wasn't a great deal of information about this little gathering. But all I needed was a date and a location. And here we are . . .'

Suddenly I understood.

'You've come back here to wipe them out,' I gasped. 'To wipe out the Agency before it can even begin.'

'Very good,' he replied. 'I'm starting to see why they recruited you. Indeed, I've come to snuff out the very first agent. And, in doing so, to extinguish the entire future of your petty, self-important organization. But what a bit of good fortune that I get to finish you off as well! Such a treat.'

'You can't do this!' I yelled. 'The Agency are important!'

'Important? You know nothing,' he snarled. 'They're cowards! Afraid of progress! Determined to control everything. Well, they could never control me!'

'You're just angry cos they kicked you out!' shouted Umer.

'A mistake that they shall never have the chance to regret,' replied Mr Malik with a cruel glint in his eye. He took another step forward.

This was it. We had no way out. Even if we turned and ran further into the cave, he'd just use his watch to freeze time. Then we'd be done for. He had all the power.

'You're wrong about the Agency,' I said. 'They've saved the world dozens of times over. If you stop them from existing, you'll kill us all!'

Again, he laughed. 'You genuinely believe that a mind as brilliant as mine can't survive anything the universe can throw at me? With this little device, I can make the world whatever I want it to be. The past, the future – all of it belongs to me now. And there's only one thing left standing in my way.'

I never saw it coming. It happened so fast. Malik just grabbed him, hurling him backwards through the gushing waterfall and into the night air. Tariq barely had a chance to cry out. And then he was gone.

'NO!' I screamed as my

legs gave way beneath me. I stumbled forward, tumbling to my knees. I felt an explosion of shock in my chest. Tears stung my eyes. The fall – the rocks – the swirling water – Tariq was gone!

A rushing sound filled my skull, the noises around me combining into a roar. Louder and louder. The raging waterfall. Malik's cruel laughter. He was staring straight at me.

Before I knew it, I was on my feet, charging towards him.

'Humza!' shouted Umer, grabbing hold of me. 'Stop! He has the watch!'

He pulled me back with all his weight and we tumbled to the floor. I was thrashing about, trying to pull myself up, but Umer wouldn't let me go.

'What on earth do you think you're doing?' said Malik through his smirk. 'Your friend is right. One click and you'll be frozen stiffer than – what was it? – a dead penguin?'

I couldn't get out of Umer's grip. I couldn't do anything. Tears ran down my cheeks. I stopped struggling and hung my head. I felt Umer relax his hold on me.

'Now,' continued Mr Malik. 'Time to tie up

loose ends. Would you prefer to jump or should I assist you, like the other chap?'

Anger exploded in me – in my head, in my stomach. To hell with his watch! I didn't care what happened. I leapt out of Umer's arms and charged towards Malik, my fists clenched. I knew I'd never reach him in time. I saw him raise his hand, lowering his thumb towards the button. I was still a foot from him when I heard the *click*.

And then . . . nothing happened. Time didn't freeze. The watch didn't work. My head crashed straight into his belly.

'*Ooooof!*' cried Mr Malik, stumbling backwards, winded.

I stumbled backwards too, surprised that I'd managed to make it to him. He looked confused . . . and furious. He jabbed the watch button again, but still nothing. He stared at it. His expression turned to shock. Even through my tears it was obvious: his watch was broken! Shattered, just like ours! The casing was dented. The glass was cracked. He couldn't use it to stop us!

'What have you done?' he yelled.

There was no time to figure it out. 'Run!' I shouted.

I grabbed Umer by the arm and we bolted straight past Mr Malik. He lunged for me, tearing at my shirt, but I pulled away. We shot out of the cave and on to the path. Down and down and down we ran . . . And all the way to the base of the falls I was filled with dread about what we might discover among the jagged rocks.

But, when we reached the bottom, there was no sign of Tariq to be found . . .

CHAPTER TWENTY-FIVE
BROKEN

'We've got to find him!' I cried as we dropped to our knees in the undergrowth, gasping for breath. 'He might still be alive.'

We'd run deeper into the woods to hide from Malik, and the sun had now vanished entirely. The forest was a single black shadow. It felt like a darkness we might never escape from.

'He's gone,' said Umer. He squeezed my shoulders, keeping me from turning back. 'He's gone.'

'It's my fault,' I sobbed, tears running down my face. 'I got him mixed up in all of this. And now, cos of me, he's . . .'

'Humza,' said Umer, squeezing my shoulder, but I shook his hand away.

'I've made everything worse. I've ruined everything. If I'd just done what I was meant to, if I'd just left that watch alone, if I'd told the Agency to arrest Malik straight away, none of this would have happened and Grandpa would still be alive.'

Umer was silent a moment.

'Maybe . . .' he began. 'Maybe it isn't over?'

'How?' I cried. 'Malik beat us. And now he's out there, looking for us. He won't let us go. We can't outsmart him. We can't escape him. He'll find us.'

'Humza,' said Umer, putting a hand on my shoulder and looking me right in the eye. 'Stop.'

And, for some reason, I stopped.

'Just breathe,' he said.

So I breathed.

'You've been getting me into trouble since I was born,' began Umer. 'I've been punished more times than I can remember because of you. If it wasn't for all the trouble you've got us into, I'd have probably never even had a detention, never been grounded, never had to give my birthday presents to the charity shop.'

'Why are you saying all this?' I sobbed.

'Because I wouldn't change any of it. It's why you're my best friend. When we're together, it's never boring. I'm friends with you because we always have adventures. We never stop doing amazing, unexpected things. I wouldn't change that, even if it meant having fewer punishments and more pocket money.'

'This is so much worse than any of that,' I said through my tears.

'It is. But you need to remember, as good as you are at getting us into trouble, you're even better at getting us out of it. You're an expert.'

'I can't . . .' I began, but Umer spoke over me.

'Listen, a minute ago you called your uncle "Grandpa".'

'So?' I sobbed.

'That means you remember him as an old man. How is that even possible if he died as a kid?'

My breathing had slowed right down as I listened to him. He was on to something. I could feel it.

'Go on,' I said.

'Maybe we're not done yet? Maybe, somehow, there's a way out of this? And, if anyone can figure it out, you can.'

'But I don't . . .' I began. 'How can I . . .?'

'Just breathe,' he said. 'Just breathe.'

I closed my eyes and breathed. All I could see

was Tariq's face. Grandpa's face. The waterfall. The drop. But then, as I began to calm a little, another image popped into my head: a flash of brass, the glint of broken glass in the lamplight . . . The watch! In all the chaos of our escape from the cave, I'd forgotten about the strange detail of the broken pocket watch.

'Malik's watch!' I shouted, looking up. 'That has to be it!'

'What do you mean?' asked Umer.

'It was broken. Shattered. That's how we managed to escape from him. He couldn't freeze time and trap us because his watch didn't work.'

'But how could it be broken if he had just used it to get here?'

'I don't know yet, but when he went to use it again, it was smashed.'

'Like our one?'

'Yeah, exactly like . . . ' The words froze on my tongue. *Our one!*

That was it! Somehow that was the answer. A thought that I couldn't quite catch hold of was swirling around my head. A weird, nonsensical, impossible thought. I *had* to check. I *had* to know.

I whipped off my backpack and opened the side

pocket – the one I'd slipped the broken watch into the day we'd arrived. It was empty.

'It's gone!' I gasped.

'Gone?' replied Umer. 'What do you mean? Did we lose it?'

'No,' I replied. 'I think . . . I think Malik has it. I think it's the one I saw in his hand just now.'

'I don't understand,' said Umer. 'If he's got our broken watch, what happened to his working one? The one he used to get here?'

'I believe this is what you are looking for,' came a voice from the undergrowth.

We spun round to see who had snuck up on us. But even when I saw his face, my brain refused to accept it. It was beyond impossible. It made no sense. It just couldn't be . . .

'Hello,' said Tariq with a small smile.

'You're alive!' I gasped, jumping to my feet and throwing my arms round him.

'I am,' he replied, laughing and hugging me back.

In an instant, Umer was beside us, crushing us both in a bear hug.

'But . . . how are you here?' I asked. 'How is it . . . How did you . . . How can . . . How?'

I couldn't put my thoughts together.

'It is OK,' said Tariq. 'Everything is OK. This is for you.'

And there in his hand was the missing pocket watch. The perfect, unbroken pocket watch that Malik had used to get here.

'But . . . how did you get that?' I asked him.

A grin spread across his face.

'*You* gave it to me.'

CHAPTER TWENTY-SIX
UMER'S SECRET

Ten minutes later, Umer and I were racing through the forest with the new, unbroken watch. Only it wasn't ten minutes later – it was an hour earlier. Confused yet? Don't worry – even Umer didn't get it and he'd been with me the whole time. You've just got to trust me, it'll all make sense soon, I promise.

'None of this . . . makes . . . sense,' panted Umer as we hurried up the slope towards the mouth of the cave.

'It makes total sense!' I shouted back over the growing noise of the waterfall. 'It's the weirdest thing ever, but it makes sense. Just wait and see!'

I felt a new energy inside me, pushing me on. Tariq had explained to us how he had survived the fall and his story had changed EVERYTHING! It was all thanks to Mr Malik's brand-new watch – the watch I now gripped tightly in the palm of my hand.

Once Tariq had shown us how the device's time-travel features worked, Umer and I had been able to use it to jump back an hour. This would give us the chance we needed to put things right once and for all. And that's why we were now reliving the same evening all over again! Wild, huh?

So, for the second time in as many hours, the sun was starting to set. The bright colours of dusk were appearing on the horizon, and it looked almost as stunning as the first time round. I can't tell you how strange it was to see the exact same sunset twice. But it was a good sign. It meant I had my timings right, and the other (earlier) versions of us would have just finished delivering Tariq's letter. Soon, they'd be on their way to the waterfall to prepare for the meeting. Which meant, for now, the cave would be completely deserted.

We were out of breath by the time we got to the top. Yellow–orange sunlight flickered through the cascading water and danced across the scattered boulders strewn about the cave.

'There,' I said, pointing towards a particularly large rock. 'That'll be perfect.'

'So you *do* want to hide behind the rocks now?' said Umer, looking pleased with himself.

'Yeah, but there's no time to be smug about it,' I replied. 'That sun's almost down and they'll be here any second.'

We dashed over to the boulder and ducked behind it. We were far enough back that, as long as we kept within the shadows, we could watch everything without being spotted. And it turned out we'd timed things perfectly: as soon as I looked out, I saw them. The other versions of ourselves had just walked in through the mouth of the cave.

'Whoa . . .' gasped Umer, peering out from his place beside me.

'I know, right . . .' I whispered. 'How weird is that?'

'Too weird,' he replied.

The other versions of us were speaking now, and I had to strain to hear what they were saying over the noise of the waterfall.

It was amazing – everything they said was exactly what we'd said first time round. It was fascinating to

watch. Or at least it was right up until the moment
I heard the most boring words in the universe:

'Wanna play I spy?' said the other Umer.

'Oh no,' I groaned, remembering what was about
to happen. We were going to have to sit through
that terrible game again. I was tempted to throw a
rock at the Umer who'd suggested it just to shut
him up. But that hadn't happened the first time
round, so I guessed I couldn't. Damn it. Thankfully,

it wasn't too long before the game was interrupted by a familiar little hooligan storming into the cave.

'You lie!' shouted my tiny dad, holding up the letter.

'Oh yeah,' whispered Umer beside me in the dark. 'I forgot about your dad showing up.'

'Yup, he's wasting our time all over again,' I replied, shaking my head. 'At least I dealt with him nice and fast.'

And I did. In less than a minute, the other version of me had grabbed my dad by the collar and marched him out of the cave. This left the other version of Umer standing there alone with a dopey look on his face. Then, as I watched him, his expression began to change. He raised an eyebrow. He glanced one way, then the other, as if to make sure he was all alone. He smiled. Something funny was going on . . .

'Uh-oh,' whispered the Umer crouching beside me.

'What's wrong?' I whispered.

'Can we not watch this next bit?' he said, ducking further behind the rock so he could no longer see his other self.

'Why not?' I asked.

'Just sit back here with me and don't watch, yeah? It's boring, I promise.'

Umer was hiding something. Now I *had* to know. I swear, though, I couldn't have guessed in a million years what was about to happen. It was spectacular.

The other Umer's toe began to tap.

'Humza, please,' whispered Umer beside me. 'Don't watch. Why don't we play I spy instead?'

'Uh-uh. I gotta see what you get up to when no one's watching . . .'

O.M.G.

I had no idea Umer had it in him. First his head began to nod. Then came the finger-clicking. Soon his hips started to go: left–right, left–right.

'Are you . . . *dancing*?' I spluttered.

But the Umer next to me wouldn't answer. He just buried his head in his hands. And that's when the singing began. Ha! It was amazing!

'Is that "Pinga"?' I whispered, stifling my laughter.

Umer could only nod, as his other self began to break into a full, well-rehearsed and expertly choreographed version of the song 'Pinga' from the movie *Bajirao Mastani*. If you ain't seen it, I wouldn't beat yourself up. I only watched it cos my family forced me. It seemed like Umer was quite the fan though.

He was really going for it – *chaff*-ing, *jhumar*-ing, *dhamal*-ing all over the place. (If you've ever seen a Bollywood film, you'll have seen that kind of dancing going on.) And, as for the singing, I gotta say, Umer didn't sound too bad. That cave had pretty good acoustics. I might have got into it myself if I hadn't been laughing so hard.

Sadly, it was over all too soon, as the other version of me arrived back just moments later. Umer's dancing halted instantly.

'What were you just doing?' asked the other Humza as he walked in.

'Uh . . . nothing . . .' said the other Umer. 'Just waiting here quietly.'

I had to cover my mouth to stop from laughing out loud. The Umer beside me shook his head, looking too embarrassed to speak.

'Don't worry,' I whispered. 'Your secret's safe with me.'

'Thanks,' grumbled Umer.

Turned out laughing at Umer was a much better way of passing the time than playing I spy, because, pretty soon, we heard movement at the mouth of the cave. Tariq had arrived. The first-ever Agency meeting was about to begin – again!

CHAPTER TWENTY-SEVEN

THE FIRST AGENCY
MEETING (AGAIN)

Now I don't need to tell you what happened next. It went exactly as it had done before. Except this time we were watching from our hiding place behind the boulder. Tariq came in, we explained everything, he asked us for proof, we convinced him, he agreed to join. And at that exact moment . . . *FLASH!*

The whole cave lit up. The ball of blue–white light appeared. And out stepped the world's most evil science teacher.

'Well, well, well,' said Mr Malik with a thin smile. 'What an unexpected treat.'

Man, I hated that guy. Behind the rock, I slipped the watch Tariq had given me from my pocket. I had to fight the urge to freeze time immediately and kick *Malik* off that cliff. But I knew how things had to play out. Tariq had told us everything we needed to do. I just had to wait until the right moment. But when it came, it was still a shock.

'And there's only one thing left standing in my way,' said Mr Malik. His expression hardly changed as he grabbed hold of Tariq. I wanted to shout out, to warn him, but I knew I couldn't. I had to let it happen. I had to watch it all over again.

Tariq was thin, his frame was light. Mr Malik was bigger and stronger. He took hold of my uncle and threw him effortlessly from the cave. The waterfall swallowed Tariq in an instant.

'NO!' screamed the other version of me, falling to his knees.

'Now!' hissed Umer beside me, gripping on to the watch in my hand.

I smashed my palm down on the FREEZE button . . .

And then there was silence. Total and utter silence.

The roar of the waterfall vanished in a heartbeat. The water pouring past the mouth of the cave appeared frozen like ice. A solid crystal wall, glowing in the purple light of the sunset.

Umer let go of his grip on the pocket watch as we stepped out from behind our rock. Even though we could see that everyone was frozen, it still felt scary approaching Mr Malik. He had that cruel grin on his face. He was looking straight at the other version of me.

I could feel the anger welling up in me again, that same anger I knew my other self was feeling right then. But this time I knew there was hope. I was going to beat Malik. I was going to save my uncle.

I ran to the edge of the cliff path and looked down towards the ground. There was Tariq, far below, just feet away from the jagged rocks. Even in the near darkness I could see the look of horror on his face, the frozen scream in his mouth. I wanted to rush down and save him straight away, but I couldn't. I had a few things to take care of first.

'Is he OK?' said Umer as I ran back into the cave.

'Yeah,' I replied. 'He's all right. Just floating there above the water.'

'What do we do now?'

'Now we nick some watches,' I said with a grin.

I ran over to where my other self was kneeling frozen in time and began to carefully unzip the side pocket of his backpack.

'What are you doing?' asked Umer. 'We need the working watch, not the broken one.'

'This is how we get it,' I said, fishing the broken pocket watch out of the bag.

I hurried over to Malik and carefully slid the working watch out of his grasp.

'Here,' I said, passing it to Umer. 'Don't drop it. That's the one we give to Tariq.'

Umer clutched it to his chest.

Next, I slipped the broken watch into Malik's hand, exactly where the other one had been. It slid into place perfectly. I knew for a fact Malik wouldn't even notice the change. Not until he tried using it, at least.

'Right,' I said to Umer. 'Time to save the day!'

Clutching the two working pocket watches, we sprinted out of the cave, down the cliff path, and over to where Tariq was suspended mid-fall.

'Man, that was too close,' I said, shaking my head.

And it really was. Tariq was less than a metre from hitting the sharp black rocks beneath. A fall like that would have meant certain death.

Umer began to take off his shoes.

'Don't worry about that,' I told him. 'They won't get wet. Look.'

With time frozen, the water wasn't behaving like you'd expect it to. The toe I'd dipped into the river wasn't absorbing moisture at all. Instead, the river seemed to just slip aside as my shoe pushed through it. It was acting more like sludge than water. It bunched up into little mounds, like a thick mud or a real nasty daal. And when I lifted my foot out the shoe was totally dry. The whole thing felt super weird.

'Come on,' I said as I hurried towards Tariq.

With his shoes still on, Umer took a careful step into the river. Then another. As soon as he realized it was OK, he chased after me. Even though the weird dry water came right up to our waists, it was still easy to move through. It just slipped round us, almost weightless.

'It's like wading through Mr Whippy,' said Umer, grinning.

'Don't get any in your pockets though,' I told him. 'It'll turn straight back into normal water when we start time again.'

Once we were far enough out, we reached

up and grabbed Tariq. When we had him safely in our arms, we guided his floating body back to the shore. We found a grassy patch on the bank and lowered him to the ground. The look on his face was pretty horrible. Total fear. I wanted to start time as soon as possible just so his fear would go away.

'Wait,' said Umer, 'won't he still be falling?'

'What do you mean?'

'Well, all we've done is take him off the water. Away from the rocks. But he's still falling fast. Now he's just going to slam into the ground *here* instead of *there*.'

It was a good point. How could we slow him down?

'Hold on . . .' I said. 'What if . . .' As I said it, I turned Tariq over – now he was facing the ground.

'Why'd you do that?' asked Umer.

'Cos now he'll be falling the other way. Straight upward.'

'Oh yeah! You've flipped the direction of his fall! That's brilliant.'

'I sure hope so,' I replied, holding up the watch. 'Here goes nothing . . .'

Click!

'*Aarghhh!*' screamed Tariq as he shot straight up in the air.

'It worked!' yelled Umer over the noise of the waterfall. 'You did it!'

'Don't get too excited,' I replied. 'We've still gotta catch him!'

When Tariq reached the top of his backwards bounce, he came to a brief stop. For just a moment, he hung there, a look of total confusion on his face. Then he began to fall. He must have been nearly twenty feet up.

'Get ready to catch him, Umer!' I yelled. 'This is gonna hurt . . .'

'*Aarrrrrgghhhhh!*'

CRASH!!!!

The three of us tumbled backwards, rolling into the undergrowth. Everything banged everything else – elbows, knees, skulls. Thankfully, Umer and I had some pretty good tummies on us to help break Tariq's fall a little.

'*Oooooofffff!*' I groaned.

'*Guughhhhhh!*' belched Umer.

'*Uuurrggghhh!*' grunted Tariq.

And then it was over. No one moved. We couldn't even breathe. The crashing sound of the waterfall filled the whole world. Tariq craned his neck up and stared at us. He looked totally and utterly stunned.

'Are you OK?' I asked him. 'Are you hurt?'

'What . . .? How . . .?' was all he could manage.

'It's all right,' I reassured him. 'Everything's gonna be OK.'

'But how did you do this?' he asked.

'Not just us,' I replied. '*You* helped too. Or at least you're going to.'

Tariq fell silent for a moment. His brain must have been doing flips trying to figure this out.

'I am very terribly confused,' he said.

'Don't worry, I'll explain everything,' I told him. 'But first we need to get out of here. Because in about thirty seconds, another me and Umer are gonna come sprinting out of that cave, and we can't be here when they do.'

Tariq nodded, even though he looked like he was barely following a word of it. I couldn't blame him. This was all too bizarre to think about for long.

'Come on,' I said, putting my arm round him and helping him up.

Umer did the same and, together, full of aches and pains, bumps and bruises, the three of us hobbled out of the clearing and into the forest.

CHAPTER TWENTY-EIGHT
ALMOST HOME

Once we'd found the spot where the other Umer and Humza would hide after their escape from Malik, I took out my version of the working pocket watch. Umer was still holding on to his one – the one we'd taken from Mr Malik in the cave – and of course it was working too. Why? Because it was the *same* watch – just an earlier version of itself! Crazy, right?

There were now two versions of the same pocket watch here, just like there were two versions of me and Umer. Thankfully, though, there was only one Mr Malik. And, because of us, he'd been left holding on to the only broken watch of the lot. Which meant we were in charge now!

I needed enough time to explain things to Tariq,

so I had him and Umer place their hands on the watch while I clicked the FREEZE button. Tariq gasped as the sounds of the forest vanished in an instant.

'We are frozen?' he asked.

'No, not us – just everything else,' I told him with a grin. 'Now listen up, this shouldn't take long.'

Tariq's brain was working like lightning as I explained everything he'd need to know. He listened quietly, nodding now and then as he took it all in. I've said it before and I'll say it again: my uncle's a pretty amazing guy. It's incredible how quickly he got to grips with it all.

The last thing I showed him was how to use the watch's time-travel controls. I wanted it to be fresh in his memory, because, in a few moments, he would have to teach the other versions of us the very same thing. Man, don't you just love a paradox?!

Now, it turned out that the little knob at the top of the watch was actually a dial. If you pulled it out a couple of millimetres, you could turn it one way or the other, letting you change the time on the main clock face. Pull it out a little further and you could change the year – found in its own little box just to the left. After you'd done that, clicking the knob back down would take you to whichever point in history you wanted to go – past, present or future.

I explained to Tariq that, moments after I restarted time, the other Umer and Humza would come stumbling into view. I described how this other Humza would start searching for the broken watch in his backpack, and at first he wouldn't understand where it had gone.

'It'll be your job to explain everything to them, just like I've explained it to you,' I told him.

'This is impossible . . .' said Tariq, shaking his head.

'Nah, it's just a paradox,' I replied with a grin. 'We've made loads of 'em and it doesn't seem to be a problem.'

'Here, you're gonna need this,' said Umer, passing Tariq the watch we'd just taken from Mr Malik. 'Careful not to drop it. They're kinda breakable . . .'

'But . . .' began Tariq, accepting the watch, 'I don't understand . . . If you taught me how to use this watch, then who taught you?'

'*You* did!' I said, laughing. 'Seriously, man, don't

overthink it. It'll give you a headache. Just tell me you get the plan.'

'I get it,' he replied. 'I will meet an earlier version of you both right here and teach you how to use this watch.' Then his expression changed. 'But . . . where will you go now?'

Something told me he already knew the answer. He just didn't want to hear it.

'We're going home,' I replied. 'We finally have a way back. And, once we're there, we can tell the Agency everything and they can clean up this whole mess.'

'The Agency . . .' said Tariq.

'Oh yeah!' I yelled. 'I can't believe I almost forgot. Here.'

I grabbed my bag and whipped out the phone and charger.

'This is for you. It's yours anyway, but now you're definitely gonna need it.'

'Mine?' he said, sounding nervous.

'This thing knows who you are, so you'll have access to everything in its database.'

'Database?' said Tariq, confused.

'Uh, yeah, it's kind of like a brain,' I explained.

'It has a brain?'

'A pretty amazing brain, actually. He ain't got much of a sense of humour but AI Akbar can tell you everything you need to know about setting up the Agency.'

'Are you certain about this?' he asked. 'I am not sure I can do what you describe.'

'Tariq,' I said, putting my hand on his shoulder, 'if anyone can do it, it's you. It might take a while, but you *will* get there. The Agency are gonna grow and grow. Get stronger and stronger. And, when you're done, you'll have saved the world more times than Umer's had hot dinners.'

'Sometimes I have double dinner,' added Umer with a grin.

Tariq looked super serious when he reached out towards me and accepted the phone.

'You know how to charge it, yeah? That Amir kid will help you – just as long as your brother doesn't scare him off.'

Tariq nodded. But there was a sadness in his eyes. 'Will I see you again?' he asked.

'Definitely,' I told him. 'After we start time again, it'll only be about thirty seconds before we come running out of the woods.'

He smiled. Grandpa's smile, with its wonky

teeth. All that wisdom and mischief and kindness. I suddenly wanted to tell him the rest. Tell him he was my uncle, tell him I'd known him my whole life. Tell him I loved him. But instead I just grabbed him.

'Thanks for everything,' I said, hugging him as hard as I could.

'Thank *you* for everything,' he replied, squeezing me back.

After he and Umer had hugged goodbye, it was time to go.

'You might wanna stand back,' I said to Tariq. 'Once I restart time, it won't be long before the other versions of me and Umer appear.'

'I will find a hiding place,' he replied with a warm smile, taking a step backwards.

I set the watch to take Umer and me back to the day we'd left the summer school. As soon as we got there, we'd run to the village, find a phone and contact the Agency. In no time at all, they'd come and clean everything up and life could finally go back to normal. Maybe my dad would still be in the village too. My proper grown-up dad. I wasn't sure how long he'd been planning to hang around, but maybe we'd find him in the marketplace buying samosas or having an argument with a taxi driver. A smile spread across my face. It was time to go home.

'Goodbye, Umer. Goodbye, Humza,' said Tariq. 'Safe travels, my friends.'

'Bye, Unc,' I said. Then I hit the button.

FLASH!

The forest vanished. The blinding light replaced everything. For an instant, the universe seemed to lose itself. And then, just as quickly, it was over. We stepped forward out of the glowing ball and back into the present day.

But the present day wasn't waiting for us. Instead, there was only a nightmare.

'What is this place?' gasped Umer.

I couldn't reply. I couldn't believe what I was seeing. Where the forest should have been, there were now only blackened husks of trees, crooked, limp and lifeless everywhere. Fires raged in the distance and smoke swirled in the dry air. The sky was like blood.

Beneath our feet, there was a sudden rumbling. I turned just in time to see a great fireball explode on the horizon. What had happened? Had I set the watch wrong? Had we travelled too far?

I checked it again. The time and date were right. We were back home. It was home that was gone. And then I heard it . . .

Chungk! Chungk! Chungk! Getting louder. Coming towards us. We turned to look. Soldiers! They were carrying weapons. But they weren't people. They were machines. And they'd spotted us.

Chungk! Chungk! Chungk! Their pace increased. The crunching of metal legs on the charred, rocky earth grew louder still.

'What *are* they?' cried Umer.

'I don't know, man, I don't know!' I replied.

And then, all at once, it was clear. When they were close enough that I could see their faces, I knew exactly what they were. Or rather *who* they were. The robots' faces were digital screens, built into their dark metallic skulls. And on each of the dozen or so head-screens was the same face.

Malik! He wasn't one man any more. He was an army. An army of robots. And look what they'd done to the world . . .

I was so shocked by the sight of the ruined planet that I wasn't thinking straight. I didn't even remember the watch in my hand and its power to stop time. The robots raised their weapons. They

must have been waiting for us here. They'd been sent to exterminate us. This was the end. I screwed my eyes up tight.

BANG! BANG! BANG! BANG! BANG!

But there was no pain. There was nothing. When I looked again, all the robots were lying in a heap on the ground. A smoking pile of machinery. 'Humza?' came a familiar voice from behind us.

I turned to see who had spoken.

No way . . .

'Grandpa?' I gasped.

And it *was* Grandpa – *old* Grandpa, with white hair and yellow teeth. But he didn't look like any version of Grandpa I'd ever seen before. He didn't look like any version of Grandpa I could ever even have imagined. This Grandpa was a soldier. A super soldier!

He was wearing a huge, battered suit of futuristic-looking armour: metal chest plate, big round shoulders, arms and legs like tree trunks. He looked massive, strong – taller, even. He was carrying a big powerful laser rifle and had a long scar running up his cheek into a black leather eyepatch.

'What the hell's going on?' I gasped.

And then he smiled. And it was *his* smile, for sure. But, somehow, it was older and more tired than I'd ever seen it.

'Welcome home, Humza,' he said.

CHAPTER TWENTY-NINE
MALIK WORLD

Grandpa was fast. His suit of armour seemed to be powered somehow, and it was making its own *kerchunk kerchunk* noise as it stomped through the wasteland that used to be a forest.

My arms and legs were still aching a bit from when young Grandpa had fallen on us from out of the sky, twenty minutes (or forty years!) earlier. Umer and I had to give it our all just to keep up.

'Where are we going, Grandpa?' I asked.

'Cave,' he replied over his shoulder.

'The cave?' said Umer. 'You mean the one behind the waterfall?'

'What waterfall?' muttered Grandpa, and, as he said it, we rounded the corner.

The waterfall was gone. The river was gone. The

banks were still there, but they were bone dry now.
There was no vegetation. No forest. No sound of
crashing water. There was only the hot dry wind
that swept across the place relentlessly.

And that's when it struck me. From here, we
ought to be able to see the village. But it was gone
too. The whole world had vanished. Or at least
everything that mattered.

'What happened, Grandpa?' I asked him as he stepped on to the path that led up the cliff face.

He paused and looked back at me.

'Malik,' he replied. 'We made a mistake.'

Before I could ask him more, he turned and marched on up the path, towards the open mouth of the cave. Once we got up there, everything looked pretty much the same. Now, though, without the water cascading past the entrance, the whole cave was filled with an eerie red light from the burning sky outside.

It felt strange to be back here so soon. So much had already taken place here. What kept bringing us back?

'Come,' said Grandpa. 'Deeper this time.'

He began to march into the darkness – much further into the cave than we'd been before. A small torch on his shoulder popped open and lit the way.

'Why?' I asked. 'What are we doing here? Why do we need to go deeper?'

'We have to stop him,' said Grandpa. 'We have to stop Malik.'

I was beginning to realize that this wasn't the Grandpa I knew. This guy was different. Hardened somehow. He'd obviously been through a lot.

'What happened, Grandpa? After we left that day, what went wrong?'

Grandpa slowed down and then stopped. He turned to face me.

'We left him. We left him in the cave,' he said. 'Right here, but in the wrong time. Not his time. We left him.'

Oh God. He was right. In all the chaos, in my desperation to get away, I hadn't thought about what would become of Malik in that cave. I guess I'd figured the Agency would just come back and clean things up once we got home. But they never got the chance. We hadn't finished the mission! And, because of us, Malik had somehow destroyed everything.

'He was already a genius in his own time,' Grandpa explained. 'But, back in the 1970s, with his advanced scientific knowledge and his understanding of technologies yet to be invented, he was more powerful than anyone on Earth. It didn't take him long to exploit this.'

'What have I done?' I gasped.

'I'd barely had time to establish the Agency when I heard about him,' Grandpa continued. 'He'd founded a company developing technologies that would not otherwise have been invented for decades to come. First he became the richest man in the world. Then the most powerful. Then he grew into something more. No one could stop him. Soon, whole countries surrendered to his control. More and more of the world fell.'

'How did you survive?' asked Umer.

'The Agency managed to gain a foothold in the time we had. We had access to advanced technology of our own. Thanks to this.' He pulled something out of a compartment near his thigh.

'The phone!' I gasped. 'You've still got it!'

'Without it, I would not be alive to meet you this day.'

'How did you find us?' asked Umer. 'How did you know we'd be here?'

'You forget, Umer,' he replied. 'I was with you when you set your watch for this date.'

'And you've remembered it all these years?' I asked.

'Of course. I have been awaiting your return.'

'But why?' I asked. 'What can *we* do now? He's destroyed the world, taken over everything. What's there left to fight for?'

'There was one technology we never had access

to. One technology we could not develop by ourselves,' replied Grandpa.

I knew immediately what he meant, what he'd been waiting for all this time . . .

'The watch!' I gasped.

He nodded.

'You have to go back,' he continued. 'Back to that day. You have to complete your mission. You have to bring Malik to justice.'

'That's why you brought us here,' I said. 'To the cave!'

Again, he nodded. This time though he was smiling the slightest of smiles.

'You are a smart boy, Humza,' he said. 'When you jump back, you will arrive at the moment you saved me from the fall. No one will see the flash, as we are now deep enough inside the cave. You must stop Malik. You must not let him leave. If you manage to do that, you will stop this future from ever coming to pass.'

Umer and I were quiet for a moment. This was big. This was bigger than we'd ever realized. This wasn't just about saving ourselves any more. The whole fate of the world rested on us getting this right.

'We'll do it,' I said to Grandpa.

'I know you will,' he replied, smiling. 'It is time.'

Hugging a guy in a suit of power armour is even less comfortable than you might imagine. It's like cuddling a Skoda. But I still squeezed him hard. It was a weird thought, but this was the one and only time I'd meet *this* Grandpa. If everything went right, if we stopped Malik and made it home, then this guy would just disappear. This version of Grandpa, the guy who'd fought his whole life just to survive, would vanish and be replaced by the Grandpa I knew and loved. Funny old Grandpa, who wore slippers to the corner shop

and drank chai out of an egg cup.

I could see by the look on his face that he knew this too. But he wasn't scared. It was a sacrifice he was ready to make. The Agency's last stand against Malik.

'Goodbye, Umer,' he said. 'I am very happy to have seen you again.'

'You too,' replied Umer, then added, 'I'm sorry we messed everything up.'

'Do not worry,' he said, grinning. 'The fight isn't over yet.'

Once I'd set the watch to take us where we needed to go, I turned to my uncle. He was slipping something out from a compartment on his belt.

'I've been keeping something for you,' he said. 'I believe this is yours.'

In his hand was the coin I'd given him all those years earlier. It had been rubbed smooth with time and handling.

'I can't believe it . . . The world ended and you still managed to hang on to that coin!' I said, laughing.

'Indeed,' he replied, grinning back at me. 'It has been my lucky charm. And now it will be yours.'

He placed the coin in my hand.

'Thanks, Grandpa,' I said. 'I'll see you real soon.'

'Safe travels,' he replied.

And, in a flash, we were gone.

We stepped out of the glowing sphere and right back into the cave. Even at this distance, I heard Tariq's cry. The cry he'd made as Malik threw him into the waterfall. We'd come back at exactly the right moment.

But this time round, I knew Tariq would be OK. Just outside the cave, an earlier version of me was about to save him from the fall. But Mr Malik didn't know that. He didn't know we were coming for him. And he didn't know that we'd never give up until we'd stopped him, once and for all.

CHAPTER THIRTY

BACK TO THE PAST

As we ran towards them, the roar of the waterfall grew louder and louder. I heard a cry. My cry. I heard Malik's laugh. The sounds echoed off the walls, ghostly and distorted. We rounded the corner just in time to see my other self crash head first into Malik's stomach.

'*Ooooof!*' cried Malik (again).

It was satisfying watching him get winded a second time. I knew we could stop him now. We just had to let the other versions of Umer and me escape, so they could go and do everything we'd just done to get back here. Then we'd show him who the real geniuses were.

'What have you done?' yelled Malik.

'Run!' yelled the other me, grabbing Umer's

arm and running for the mouth of the cave.

We saw Malik lunge forward, but he clearly hadn't got his breath back yet. He stumbled, barely managing to stay on his feet. He let out a growl of frustration as he turned. And that's when he saw us, walking towards him from the darkness of the cave.

'Don't even think about moving,' I said, holding up the pocket watch.

Malik glanced at his own watch – the broken one clasped in his hand – then looked back at me. I could see him work it all out in an instant, see him understand how we'd got the better of him.

He smiled. 'Very good . . .' he said, impressed. 'You really won't quit, will you?'

'I've got a mission to complete,' I replied. 'I'm taking you in.'

'Is that what you think?' he said, still smiling.

'Just freeze him,' growled Umer. 'We win, you lose. It's over.'

'And what do you think happens next, hmm?' he asked. 'You take me back to the present, hand me in to the Agency, and then what?'

'They lock you up,' I replied.

'Exactly,' said Malik, that devilish grin of his spreading across his face. 'Instead of finishing me off like they ought to, they'll lock me away. Or at least they'll try to.'

Suddenly I knew he was up to something. He was out-thinking us right then and there – ten moves ahead!

I didn't even have time to process the thought before a flash of light exploded in my vision. I spun round just in time to see another Mr Malik step into the cave. The pulsing ball of blue–white energy vanished behind him. He looked a little older than the original Malik. He had a streak of grey in his hair. In one hand he was carrying some sort of high-tech laser rifle and, in the other, a brand-new pocket watch!

'And lock me up they did,' said this new version of Mr Malik, grinning. 'But, of course, I escaped.'

What?! Could it really be?! Was this guy another Malik, from even further in the future?

'How . . .?' I gasped.

'Do you really think your precious Agency could keep someone as brilliant as *me* locked up for long?' said future Malik, raising his gun. 'It was only a matter of time before I broke free. And the first thing I did was build another watch.'

I was still holding our version of the pocket

watch. He was holding his. I could get my thumb to the button in under a second. But that gun was pointed straight at me. It would be close. Too close. But what choice did I have?

Just as I was about to press it, he spoke.

'You're thinking of pressing that button, aren't you, Humza?' said future Malik, grinning. 'Go right ahead. It won't help you. It won't do anything at all. You see, I've made some improvements to my design.'

And, as he said it, the face of his watch popped open, exposing the heart of the machinery. Inside was a pulsing yellow ring of light.

'No more time-freezing for you,' he continued. 'This little component makes sure of that. Go ahead and see if I'm lying.'

I knew he was telling the truth, but I had to see. I clicked the button. Nothing happened. I clicked again. Still nothing.

Both Maliks began to laugh. That ugly, cruel sound bounced around the walls of the cave.

'Oh dear, boys,' said the original Malik. 'It looks like it's all over. I told you, you should have finished me off instead of locking me up.'

'You'll not get that chance again, I'm afraid,'

added future Malik, aiming his weapon at me. 'Goodbye, Humza. You put up a brave fight.'

And then came the flash. A blinding light that, for an instant, I thought must be the laser. I was certain I was a goner. But then I heard a voice. My voice! But it wasn't me. It was coming from ten feet away . . .

'Fight ain't done yet!' said the voice.

I turned round just in time to see a future version of myself dive out of a time bubble and roll behind a boulder. He was carrying a big futuristic-looking blaster of his own and immediately started firing off a volley of laser shots.

Future Malik dived for cover and started firing back. I grabbed Umer and pulled him to the floor, behind a big rock. Original Malik threw himself behind another large boulder a few metres away.

'Hey, Humza!' yelled the other version of me between laser blasts. 'It's me, future Humza! I'm you, but from a bit further down the line! How's it going?'

'Uh, pretty weird to be honest,' I shouted back.

'Ha!' He laughed. 'I know, I totally remember. Don't worry, we've got this.'

'What the hell's going on?' I shouted.

They were still shooting at each other, and Umer and I were doing our best to keep our heads down.

'Well,' continued future Humza, 'this guy Malik is turning out to be a real pain in the backside. The Agency locked him up, but he just broke straight out and built himself a new time machine. So now I've come back to help you stop him.'

'Oh right . . . thanks,' I shouted to my other self, not knowing what else to say.

'Two Humzas and two Maliks,' said Umer. 'This should be an interesting fight.'

'What you talking about?' I replied. 'You can't just leave it to us Humzas! You gotta fight too!'

'No way,' said Umer, shaking his head. 'There's only one Umer in this cave and he's staying put.'

But, before I could argue with him further, another time bubble burst into existence. Out of it stepped yet another Malik. This one was wearing some sort of blue power armour. He looked huge. Both his arms were laser cannons and every step he took shook the cave. He began firing immediately.

'Ah, come on!' I shouted. 'That ain't fair! How many Maliks are gonna show up?'

'Don't worry,' said Umer, pointing. 'Look, reinforcements.'

I turned to see another Humza come running out of a time bubble and into the cave. This future-future version of me had his own bright red suit of power armour. It had cannons and lasers and all sorts built into it, as well as some kind of rocket-powered wheelies on the feet. Future-future me jetted into the fight on his roller-shoes, firing off a dozen tiny missiles from one arm and a laser blast from the other.

'Hey, Humza!' future-future me shouted. 'I'm another you, but from even further in the future! Our first attempts to stop Malik didn't work. He escaped again. That's why the Agency built us this power armour to even things up. Pretty sick, huh?'

'Looks great!' I shouted. 'I think I'm just gonna hide back here with my cowardly mate though!'

'Ha!' Future-future me laughed as he jetted past, firing off a bunch of mini missiles. 'I can't blame you. Hey, Umer!'

And, no sooner had he said it, than another bright flash lit the walls. A fourth Malik came charging out of a time bubble and into the cave. This one had a fully robotic body, but with a human head. He must have been nine feet tall.

'You may have destroyed my body in this fight,'

said this version of Malik, 'but you can never destroy my genius!'

And then he started shooting too.

'This is ridiculous!' yelled Umer over the chaos.

'I know!' I cried. 'How many more are gonna show up?'

And, even during that short conversation, like five more Maliks and Humzas had appeared. One Malik had the body of a robot spider. There was a Humza with a big scar on his face and another with a jetpack. There were three little Malik clones with high-pitched voices that ran out of the same time bubble, and I even saw an old-man Humza from far in the future, with white hair and a beard.

This was nuts! Humzas and Maliks from further and further into the future just kept showing up to fight one another. More and more time bubbles were appearing every few seconds. There must have been fifty of 'em at least. The cave was beginning to fill up. This couldn't end well!

'What do we do, Humza?' said Umer, and he looked genuinely scared.

'I don't know, man,' I shouted back. 'I don't think we can stop this! It's like every time one of them comes close to losing, they just jump back to their own time, develop better weapons and dive back into the fight.'

'They're gonna destroy everything!' shouted Umer.

He was right. There was only one way this could go. Total destruction. And that's when it hit me. You can't solve a problem like this with fighting. *Sometimes, when dealing with a bully, the only option is to outsmart them . . .*

There was only one thing that could stop this fight. Only one person who could end it. And, to be honest, I doubted even that would work. But I had to try. It was our only hope.

'Umer,' I said as I fiddled with the watch. 'If this

works, I'll be right back.'

'What are you . . .' he began, but I didn't stick around to let him finish the sentence.

I leapt out from behind our boulder, right into the middle of the battle. A laser blast exploded at my feet, a rocket whizzed past my head. I didn't stop. I dived into a roll, then leapt back up again. I could see the robot-spider version of Malik above me, dashing across the ceiling. He'd spotted me and was about to leap. But I jumped first. I flew through the air, arms outstretched.

Original Mr Malik, crouching behind his rock, only had a moment to look up before I slammed into him. The second that watch touched him, I jammed my thumb down on the button.

In an instant, there was nothing but white light. The sound of the battle vanished, the universe tripped and tumbled over itself, and my summer-school science teacher and I bounced out of the 1970s and into the distant future . . .

CHAPTER THIRTY-ONE
WORLD'S END

We rolled out of the time bubble and on to the floor of the cave. There was total silence. The battle was over – it had been for more than a hundred years.

I jumped to my feet and held the watch up so Malik could see it. I didn't need to tell him I'd freeze time if he tried anything. His watch was still broken, mine wasn't. He knew I was in control.

'Where have you taken me?' he demanded. 'When is this?'

'Come and see,' I replied, stepping backwards.

'See what?' he snarled.

'What you made. What you created with all your genius.'

He didn't reply. He just stared at me a moment, then pulled himself to his feet. I began edging backwards towards the mouth of the cave – towards where the waterfall had once been. When Malik arrived at the cliff face, his jaw dropped. He stopped dead in his tracks and stared out at the world before him.

'It's gone . . .' he said. 'It's all gone.'

And he was right. From up here, so high above the ground, the view of the wasteland was horrifying. Everything was dead. The swirling, angry red sky was like some image of hell. The rivers were gone. The trees were burned. The village was reduced to dust.

'This is all that's left,' I told him. 'This is what we get if we keep fighting this fight.'

He didn't reply. He just stared out at the ruined world in front of him.

'You don't want this,' I went on. 'I know you don't. No one could want this. But this is what happens if we don't stop ourselves going down that path. We can't beat you. You're too smart. But you can't beat us either. So we all lose.'

'But . . . how?' he eventually murmured. 'How does it come to this?'

'You saw it for yourself. That fight back there just keeps on going. You make a move, we make a move right back. Bigger weapons, more destruction. And this is where we end up. All of us.'

He said nothing. He just stared out at the dead world.

'You can't let this happen,' I told him. 'You're too smart to be that stupid.' But it was like he couldn't even see me any more. Couldn't hear me. I knew I had to get through to him.

'Years ago,' I continued, 'when the Agency tried to control your research, this is what they were trying to prevent. Even with that giant brain of yours, it was the one thing they could see that you couldn't. But it doesn't have to be this way. You can still stop it.'

He looked away. Turned his back to the dead landscape. He was staring into the darkness of the cave. The walls were blackened with laser blasts and battle scars. It must have been a hell of a fight.

'This is on you,' I said as I reset the pocket watch. 'You've gotta decide what happens next. No one's trying to control you any more. No one's telling you what to do. It's your call. I just hope you make the right decision.'

I held my hand out towards him. He stared at it a moment. At the pocket watch in my palm. Then he reached towards me. And, in a flash of light, we vanished.

The battle was raging as we stepped out of the bubble. I knew we only had a moment before a missile or a laser blast would take us down. It was now or never.

All around us, Humzas and Maliks fought one another. Explosions shook the cave every second. The waterfall roared behind us. Beside me, Mr Malik stared silently at it all. The cruel smile was gone. His eyes were full of sadness. That superhuman brain of his had slowed right down. He wasn't just racing through every possible option and outcome any more, looking for the next move. He was feeling it.

I saw Umer crouching behind a nearby boulder, staring straight at me. Just a few metres from that, I could see one of the Maliks heading straight for him. I saw another one coming for me, robotic hands outstretched. I knew this was it. One way or another, it was all about to end. I closed my eyes. Oh well, it was worth a try . . .

'STOP!'

The voice exploded from right beside me.

Malik's voice. So loud, so powerful that everything else was suddenly silenced. I opened my eyes to see every other Humza and Malik staring at us. For just a heartbeat, it was as though time had frozen. We all stared at one another. And then they began to vanish. Each and every last one of them suddenly popping out of existence.

It was amazing! With that single decision, Mr Malik had changed everything. In the blink of an eye, that war-filled future had ceased to exist. The fight was over before it could begin.

The cave was suddenly empty again. Umer looked out from behind his boulder.

'So . . . um . . . it worked then?' he said with a nervous smile.

I nodded, smiling back at him. It was only then that I realized I was still holding Mr Malik's hand, the pocket watch sandwiched between our palms. We let go of our grip on one another. I looked up at him.

'There'll be no more fighting,' he said softly. 'Not from me.'

'You'll come back with us then?' I asked. 'Talk to the Agency?'

He nodded.

'I'm glad to hear it,' I said, turning to my friend. 'What do you reckon, Umer? You about ready to go home?'

A grin spread across his face.

'No time like the present,' he replied.

After I had prepped the watch to take us home, I held it out towards the others.

'Here goes . . .' I said.

Umer and Mr Malik placed their hands on top of mine. A click, a flash, a rush of noise . . . and we were back.

We stepped out of the ball of crackling light and into the familiar cave. Now, though, sunshine poured in through the waterfall. I don't know how I knew it – how I was so sure of it – but we were home. This was our world. Our time.

The noise of the waterfall made it impossible to hear what was going on out in the clearing, but the moment we stepped from the cave, it became apparent we weren't alone. The Agency had been waiting for us. And they'd shown up in force.

Helicopters, tanks, jeeps, soldiers. They were putting on a show of strength. I guess it was understandable: they didn't know Malik would be

turning himself in. He looked a little wary as we stepped on to the ledge.

'It'll be OK,' I said to him. 'They just want to talk.'

He nodded, but said nothing. I think he was still in shock about how he'd destroyed the world. Fair enough, really. That's never a cool move.

'Congratulations, Agent Badman,' came a nearby voice. 'Mission accomplished.'

I looked up to see Agent Akbar walking towards us. I'd got so used to seeing him as just a floating head that it was kind of weird to see him with a body again.

'Agent Akbar!' I yelled. 'You came to welcome us home! See, Mr Malik, I told you the Agency were nice guys.'

'Handcuff him,' said Akbar to the burly agents standing behind him.

'He's coming peacefully,' I told the agents as they approached. 'He chose this.'

Mr Malik didn't resist as they slipped him into the handcuffs.

'Come, Agent Badman, you can explain everything,' said Agent Akbar, patting me on the shoulder.

'Tell you what,' I replied, 'how about I fill you in on the flight?'

'Flight?' he said, looking puzzled. 'Where are we going?'

'Eggington,' I replied. 'We got a school to vandalize.'

CHAPTER THIRTY-TWO
CLOWN TIME

It turns out the Agency are pretty damn helpful once they know you basically created 'em. They did anything we asked them to: drove us around, flew us back to England on a private jet. It was pretty gangsta.

Once we'd got home, we jumped back to the last day of primary school and tagged up the canteen, making sure we were right under the CCTV camera as we did it. We had to set everything in motion exactly as it had been. We had to get in trouble, get punished and wind up in Pakistan just as we had before. The mission wouldn't be complete until we were done.

After vandalizing the canteen, we jumped forward a week to post the summer-school flyer through the door. We arrived at the exact moment everyone was inside, yelling at us.

'So I guess we *were* to blame for the graffiti after all,' said Umer as I popped the flyer through the letterbox.

'Yup,' I replied, grinning. 'Looks like our parents were right to punish us. We could really do with some discipline.'

We both began to laugh as we wandered back down the path. Even from the street, we could hear the raised voices coming from inside the house. Those other versions of us being shouted at right now had no idea of the adventure they were about to go on . . .

Within twenty-four hours, we were back in Pakistan, soaring over the forest in a slick black helicopter.

'I'm still confused,' said Umer as the chopper tore over the treetops. 'Why do we even have to go back to summer school? The mission's done. We won. Can't we just time-travel to the end of the month and miss the whole summer-school thing altogether?'

'No can do,' I replied. 'If we skip those three weeks, it'll look like we've just vanished. The school will probably think we're dead or something. You don't want your mum and dad worrying like that, do you?'

'No,' replied Umer. 'I guess not.'

We touched down in a clearing a couple of minutes up the road from the school.

'Excellent work, boys,' shouted Agent Akbar over the noise of the engine. 'Malik is in custody, but he is cooperating. You did a first-class job.'

'Cheers, Agent Akbar,' I said, putting on my rucksack. 'I'll give you a call some time when I'm back. You know, if I'm not too busy.'

Agent Akbar grinned. 'I look forward to it,' he said, and I could see he meant it.

We jumped out into the sunshine, then watched the helicopter take off again. When it was quiet enough to speak, Umer turned to me and sighed.

'Three full weeks of studying?' he said, clearly still trying to convince me to find another option.

'Afraid so,' I replied, fishing out the pocket watch and adjusting the date. 'You ready?'

He nodded and placed his hand on mine. I hit the button . . .

FLASH!

The world flashed bright and, in an instant, we were back. Back on that same day Umer and I had first jumped through time. I was getting so used to the sensation of time travel that it didn't even feel that weird any more.

'I reckon I'm a bit of a natural when it comes to time travel,' I said to Umer as we strolled up the hill. 'Maybe after I'm done being a spy I can be the first brown Doctor Who.'

'Your parents would like that,' he replied with a grin. 'Asian parents love a doctor.'

'Ha, yeah, even a dentist would do. Dentist Who.'

'Accountant Who,' Umer said, giggling.

'Married-But-Still-Living-At-Home Who.'

'Ha ha!' Umer laughed. 'That show would be super popular with Asian mums and dads.'

'See?' I said as we approached the bend that led to the school's entrance. 'We're laughing already. I'm sure the next three weeks won't be that bad.'

I tell you, though, I was not prepared for what was waiting for us round that corner. The school building was still there, exactly as we'd left it, but everything else had changed. The black-and-white sign by the entrance gate was gone. In its place was a huge purple-and-green banner, which read WELCOME TO SUMMER CAMP!

'Summer *camp*?' said Umer, looking confused.

Kids were running around everywhere. There were boys and girls flying kites, others playing games of cricket. There was even a clown! 'O.M.G. Is that . . .' I said.

'It totally is . . .' replied Umer.

'Hello, boys!' chuckled the clown, a huge smile on his painted face. 'We are about to have a water-balloon fight! Come and join us!'

'Mr Mahmood?' I gasped, unable to believe it could be true.

Where was the horrible strict headmaster we'd left behind a week ago? Who was this . . . clown?

'What's happened?' said Umer. 'What's going on?'

'I don't know,' I replied. 'I don't get how this is possible . . .'

It didn't take us long to discover the answer . . .

Half an hour after we'd arrived, while we were exploring this new fun version of the school, we walked past Mr Mahmood's office. At first I didn't notice anything and was about to leave. But then something caught my eye. I did a double take.

'Umer, check this out,' I shouted.

The little room was still filled with pictures of Mr Mahmood, but now every single one of them had changed. No longer was he all alone. Now there were friends and family in every photo. No more holidays by himself, no more lonely trips to the zoo or the park. He was surrounded by loved ones. He looked happy.

And then I spotted it. Right in the middle of the back wall. A little bald boy standing next to another kid – a very familiar kid. They were each holding a cricket bat and grinning at the camera.

'Wait – is that your dad?' gasped Umer. 'And is he with . . .'

'Amir!' I replied. 'Amir Mahmood!'

'Amir's the headmaster?' said Umer, wide-eyed.

'Yeah!' I laughed. 'He and my dad became friends!'

'That means you changed history!' said Umer, laughing. 'You made the headmaster nice.'

'Ha! I guess I did,' I replied, totally unable to believe that being friends with *my dad* was enough to make any little boy turn nice. But I guess a best friend can make a lot of difference to you when you're that age. Mine definitely had. I turned to Umer and saw that he was wearing the same stupid grin on his face as me. Man, I was lucky he'd come on this adventure.

'What are you two so happy about?' came a familiar voice behind us.

'Azrah!' I shouted when I saw her.

'King Kong!' shouted Umer when he spotted the kitten she was holding.

'Man, it's great to see you,' I said.

'Both of you,' added Umer, tickling King Kong under her little chin.

'Hey, aren't you worried about getting caught

with her in the hall?' I asked Azrah, looking about.

'Why would I be worried?' she replied. 'Mr Mahmood loves these kittens.'

'Does he?' I said, laughing. 'I should have guessed.'

'Hey, Azrah, you wanna come exploring with us?' asked Umer.

'Always,' said Azrah, grinning. 'Maybe we will discover more secret tunnels.'

'Or even a top-secret laboratory,' I added.

'A what?' she asked.

'Don't worry about it,' I replied, grinning back at her. 'Let's just have some fun.'

And, with that, the three of us set off down the corridor together, to see what adventures our summer camp had in store.

I gotta tell you, we had the best three weeks ever. The place was amazing. We did so many awesome activities. Rock climbing, kayaking, fire building, archery . . . At night, we told stories round the camp fire and cooked our own food, right there under the stars. We found out about all the local animals, and saw a few of them too (no more dinosaurs, thankfully). I even began to improve my Urdu a bit. I couldn't wait to show it off to my mum – I knew she'd cry, but in a good way.

It had been over a month since we'd first left England and I was definitely ready to go home. But what was weird was that, for the first time in my whole life, Pakistan kind of felt like home now too.

CHAPTER THIRTY-THREE

HOMEWARD BOUND

We were standing by the main entrance of the summer camp, in the very same spot my dad had dropped us off a month earlier. Other kids had been getting into cars and on to buses all morning and now, apart from Azrah, who was still saying goodbye to her cats, Umer and I were the only ones left.

Azrah's mum was waiting beside their car with her arms crossed and an impatient look on her face. Azrah was in the middle of cuddling Chooha, the mother cat, and her four kittens for the fiftieth time that morning.

'Mr Mahmood has agreed to let them stay,' she said, looking up at us with a huge grin. 'I cannot wait to come back next year and see how big they've grown.'

'That's great news,' I told her. 'Hopefully we can come back then and see them too. And . . . you know . . . you.'

'I would like that very much,' she said, blushing a little.

'If you're gonna kiss her, now's your chance, double-0-sensitive,' whispered Umer with a grin.

'Shut up,' I hissed, elbowing him in the ribs before turning back to Azrah. 'You've got our addresses, yeah?'

'Of course,' she replied. 'I will write to you the moment I get home.'

The kittens mewed as she jumped into her mum's car and rumbled off in a cloud of dust, waving all the way down the road. As the noise of the car engine faded, it was replaced by the mosquito hum of a distant motorcycle rickshaw.

'Do you think that's him?' asked Umer.

'I hope so,' I replied. 'Cos if he's forgotten, we've got a long walk back to England.'

A moment later, there was a crunch of gravel and a screech of tyres, as the same ugly little vehicle that had dropped us off came skidding to a halt in front of the entrance.

'My boys!' cried Dad, leaping out of the rickshaw

so violently that it almost toppled over backwards behind him. He grabbed me in the biggest hug he'd ever given me, lifting me right off the ground. It was weird – he actually seemed happy to see me! I should go away for a month more often.

'Hi, Abu-jee,' I said, squeezing him back.

'Hi, Mr Khan,' said Umer as my dad reached out and pulled him into the hug.

'My dear friend!' came a cry from behind us.

As soon as he heard it, my dad pretty much dropped me and Umer in the dirt. He threw open his arms and ran towards the school. There in the doorway stood Amir Mahmood with a huge grin on his face.

'Amir!' shouted my dad, hugging his friend. 'Your hair has still not arrived, I see?'

'Ha!' Mr Mahmood laughed. 'And I notice your puppy fat remains stubbornly present.'

Then they both laughed and hugged each other again.

'So, you remember each other now then, do you?' I asked.

'What?' replied my dad, flashing me a confused look. 'Of course we do! You would not forget Umer just because you did not see him for a month, would you?'

'Just checking,' I said with a grin.

'Your son is peculiar, my friend,' added Mr Mahmood. 'Just like his father.'

'At least I have a son, you lonely old goat!' replied my dad.

There was a moment's silence as the two men stared at each other. Then they both burst out laughing and hugged again.

'These two are weird,' said Umer.

'Yup,' I replied. 'Let's never end up like that.'

After we'd said our goodbyes to Mr Mahmood and loaded up the rickshaw, we began our journey home.

We'd only made it five minutes down the hill when I turned to my dad.

'Abu-jee,' I said, 'maybe, if there's time, we could go see the village you came from? Just for a bit? I'd like to see it with you.'

He didn't reply at first; he just stared at me. But there was something soft in it. Something warm and sad and happy – a whole mix of things I'd not seen before.

'I would like that very much,' he said with a smile.

Then he leaned forward and tapped the driver on the shoulder. He gave the man some instructions in Urdu, and pretty soon we were skidding our way down the path that led to the village.

'Now,' said my dad, leaning in close to me as if to whisper a secret. 'If there's time, I will show you something very special. Just outside my village is the most beautiful waterfall in all the world. And hidden behind it, there is a secret cave!'

'It sounds amazing, Abu-jee,' I told him. 'I can't wait to see.'

'I discovered it!' he said, thrusting one finger into the air. 'It is where I first killed a skeleton!'

'I'd like to hear that story, Dad,' I told him, resting my head on his shoulder.

The sunlight through the trees flickered across my eyelids, as we hurtled down the path, listening to Dad's wild tales. And, who knows, if my own adventures in the village were anything to go by, maybe it was true after all.

As we walked through the arrivals gate, I heard a great big cheer. Everyone was there! Mum, Grandpa, Auntie Uzma, Umer's mum and dad, even Wendy Wang had come along with her mum, Linda.

When my mum got hold of me, she came *this* close to squeezing me to death with her bear hug.

'*Meh aap ko bohot yaad kher rahah ta*, amee jee,' I said to her when I could breathe again (which basically means 'I missed you, Mum' in Urdu).

A look of total shock fell across her face. Then she burst into tears. The good kind. The hug she gave me after that was one of the biggest I'd ever had – and I've hugged a guy in power-armour!

Umer and his little Ewok parents were hugging too, and everyone else was queuing up for their turn.

'Welcome back!' cried Wendy, pushing her way

to the front. 'How was Pakistan?'

'It was amazing!' I told her. 'How was maths camp?'

'Excellent, thanks. I can do algebra now,' she replied.

'I don't know what that is, but I'm happy for you,' I said, grinning.

Grandpa and Auntie Uzma were hanging back quietly, waiting their turn for a hug. As soon as I could, I ran over and threw my arms round them both.

'Ooooohhh!' squealed Auntie Uzma, squeezing my cheeks. 'So, you enjoyed your time in Pakistan, did you, darling?'

'I loved it, Auntie,' I told her. 'I'm definitely going back.'

'Welcome home, Humza,' said Grandpa softly.

He had a strange smile on his face – I couldn't quite read it. There was so much I wanted to say and to ask him, so much I needed to know about what had happened after we'd left him at the waterfall all those years ago. Had he worked out who I was? Did he know this whole time that I was the kid from the village? And just how the hell had he managed to set up the Agency all by himself? I had so many questions, but I couldn't ask a single one of them with everyone here.

'Do not worry,' said Grandpa as though he was reading my mind. 'We will speak properly soon. Thanks to you, we have all the time in the world.'

After we'd sat down at the airport cafe and shared every summer-camp story we could think of (or at least the ones that hadn't been classified as top secret), we headed to the multi-storey carpark.

'Do you two want to hang out together tomorrow?' asked Wendy from the window of her mum's car. 'There's still a week left before school starts.'

'Definitely,' replied Umer from his own car as he fiddled with his seatbelt. 'Meet in the park after breakfast?'

'Yeah, boi,' I said, standing between the two of them. 'We got some serious catching up to do.'

'Bye bye, boys!' called Linda Wang with a wave as she pulled away. 'Glad you are home safe!'

'*Byyyeee!*' yelled Wendy out of her window as they sped off.

As I watched her go, I knew straight away that I was gonna tell Wendy everything that had happened. Not telling Umer they'd made me a spy was one of the biggest mistakes of my life. I wouldn't have survived without him. I was never gonna keep anything from my best friends again. Being a kid ain't easy. We were gonna have to get through it together. And that meant no more secrets.

'Thanks for everything,' I said, turning back to Umer.

'You too,' he replied through the open window. 'It's been . . . an adventure.'

'It sure has!' I said, laughing. 'Imagine what next year's gonna bring.'

'You know what?' he replied. 'I think we can handle it. Once you've been chased by dinosaurs, how bad can big school really be?'

★

On the drive home, Grandpa leaned over to me.

'I have something of yours,' he said, reaching into his bag.

'You don't still have it, do you?' I asked.

It was even more yellow and cracked and rubbish-looking than ever. It was now officially the oldest mobile phone in the universe.

'Did you know this whole time?' I asked him.

'I had my suspicions when you were little,' he replied, grinning. 'But defeating those aliens confirmed it. That is how I knew you were ready to join the Agency.'

He held the phone out for me to take.

'You know what?' I replied, putting my hand on top of the mobile and pushing it back towards him. 'I think I'm gonna pass. You should probably take this and all.'

I slipped my hand into my pocket and pulled out the pocket watch.

'Tell Agent Akbar I appreciate everything, but I don't think I'm ready to be a spy just yet. I ain't done being a kid.'

Grandpa smiled, but said nothing.

'This whole mess came about because I just had to muck around with that watch. It could have all been avoided if I'd just been a good, serious, well-behaved spy. And I know now - that's the last thing I want. I'm too young to be so serious! I want to mess around. I want to annoy the neighbours, break windows, get chased out of McDonald's for starting a food fight. I want to accidentally cause a fire while trying to build a robot. I want to break my arm while skateboarding off the shed roof. And, because of all those reasons and a lot more, I've decided I'm gonna pass on the whole spy thing. For now at least.'

I handed Grandpa the watch. He accepted it silently, resting it in his lap beside the phone. Then he looked up at me with that brilliant piano-key grin of his.

'I think you are more wise than you know, Agent Badman,' he said. 'The Agency thanks you for your service.'

And, just like that, I was free. No more responsibilities, no more punishments. Nothing but a whole week of summer holiday to enjoy. And, with the way things had been going lately, who knew how much trouble I could get into in that time? But there was one thing I was sure of: I was gonna have fun finding out.

ACKNOWLEDGEMENTS

Firstly, a big thank you to all the teachers who put up with us over the years without ever once trying to destroy the world. Appreciate it.

A great big thanks to our parents for a lifetime of support, and for always being willing to look at early drafts as this book came together.

Massive thanks to Humza's manager, Dhanny Joshi, his agent, Matilda Forbes-Watson, and to Henry's agent, Sean Gascoine.

Thanks to our guinea-pig readers, Mabel Treglown, Florence Taylor and Stanley Hurst. (They're not actually guinea pigs – they're human children.)

Thanks to Dan, Clare, Enara & Amaia Breeze for providing a room to write in for so long.

A special thanks to our editors, Holly Harris, Sharan Matharu and Tom Rawlinson, for all their hard work and support throughout this process. And to Shreeta Shah for locating and correcting our single spelling mistake ;-)

Thanks to our proofreaders Claire Davis and Marcus Fletcher for all their work getting things in order, and Waleed Akhtar for helping make sure we didn't offend anyone!

Thanks to Roz Hutchison for getting the book out there and making some noise about it. And to all the rest of the incredible team at Puffin Books who have helped get this next book finished – thanks a million.

A massive thanks to Aleksei Bitskoff for his brilliant illustrations, and Andrea Kearney for your excellent design work. You've made this book look even more beautiful than Humza claims to be (and that's quite a feat).

And last but not least, a huge thank you to every kid who chooses to read this book instead of robbing a bank or stealing a space rocket (or whatever it is kids do these days when they're not reading). We hope you enjoy the story.

 What began with making funny videos in his bedroom (107 million viewers, but who's counting?), has led **Humza Arshad** to become a children's author, an ambassador for YouTube and The Prince's Trust, and to produce his own scripted comedies for BBC Three, the mockumentary series Coconut and *Jumpers* for Sky Comedy. Humza is an anti-hate activist, speaking regularly at events around the world – including a recent address at the UN, alongside Whoopi Goldberg and Queen Rania of Jordan. His mum is really proud.

Follow Humza on Twitter, Snapchat and Instagram
@HumzaProduction

and on YouTube
@HumzaProductions

**Henry White** is a comedy writer working in television and children's fiction. He grew up in west London and began his career in online animation. Henry went on to write and direct adverts for a number of British comedy channels, before working as a sitcom writer. He has a birthmark shaped like a duck.

BEFORE THE TIME-TRAVELLING TEACHER OF DOOM THERE WAS . . .

School has got really weird. All the teachers are disappearing and the aunties are taking over. For Humza, Umer and Wendy, it wasn't too bad at the start – the aunties just kept feeding them delicious snacks.

But now it's clear something big and bad is going on. And it's up to Humza and his friends to put a stop to it!

READ THE FIRST HILARIOUS LITTLE BADMAN ADVENTURE

WANT EVEN MORE LITTLE BADMAN, ALONG WITH MORE AMAZING STORIES?

TRY *THE PUFFIN BOOK OF BIG DREAMS*.
A book celebrating 80 years of Puffin, which includes the story 'Little Badman's Big Dream', along with many other tales from the world's best story-tellers!